4/1

What on earth was wrong with her?

She had always shied away from transitory affairs, and this could be nothing more than that. And she was breaking all her rules about getting involved with a work colleague.

The thought should have brought her back to some semblance of sanity, but it didn't. The trouble was that right at this moment she didn't care about any of that. She wanted him. In fact she couldn't remember ever wanting any man this badly.

So what if he was a work colleague and probably a philanderer...? What the heck? she thought as she stood on tiptoe to kiss him again. He would be going back to Barbados in a week.

Just how many complications could one man stir up in a week?

GW00703323

Kathryn Ross was born in Zambia, where her parents happened to live at that time. Educated in Ireland and England, she now lives in a village near Blackpool, Lancashire. Kathryn is a professional beauty therapist, but writing is her first love. As a child she wrote adventure stories, and at thirteen was editor of her school magazine. Happily, ten writing years later, DESIGNED WITH LOVE was accepted by Mills & Boon®. A romantic Sagittarian, she loves travelling to exotic locations.

Recent titles by the same author:

THE FRENCHMAN'S MISTRESS
A LATIN PASSION
A SPANISH ENGAGEMENT
THE ITALIAN MARRIAGE

THE MILLIONAIRE'S SECRET MISTRESS

BY
KATHRYN ROSS

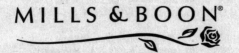

MILLS & BOON®

To my editor Kate, with thanks

DID YOU PURCHASE THIS BOOK WITHOUT A COVER?

If you did, you should be aware it is **stolen property** as it was reported *unsold and destroyed* by a retailer. Neither the author nor the publisher has received any payment for this book.

All the characters in this book have no existence outside the imagination of the author, and have no relation whatsoever to anyone bearing the same name or names. They are not even distantly inspired by any individual known or unknown to the author, and all the incidents are pure invention.

All Rights Reserved including the right of reproduction in whole or in part in any form. This edition is published by arrangement with Harlequin Enterprises II B.V. The text of this publication or any part thereof may not be reproduced or transmitted in any form or by any means, electronic or mechanical, including photocopying, recording, storage in an information retrieval system, or otherwise, without the written permission of the publisher.

This book is sold subject to the condition that it shall not, by way of trade or otherwise, be lent, resold, hired out or otherwise circulated without the prior consent of the publisher in any form of binding or cover other than that in which it is published and without a similar condition including this condition being imposed on the subsequent purchaser.

MILLS & BOON and MILLS & BOON with the Rose Device are registered trademarks of the publisher.

First published in Great Britain 2005
Harlequin Mills & Boon Limited,
Eton House, 18-24 Paradise Road, Richmond, Surrey TW9 1SR

© Kathryn Ross 2005

ISBN 0 263 84164 2

Set in Times Roman 10½ on 11½ pt.
01-0705-52134

Printed and bound in Spain
by Litografia Rosés, S.A., Barcelona

CHAPTER ONE

'I BELIEVE you're going speed dating tonight?'

The casual question was asked just as Lucy was preparing to go into the boardroom to deliver what could possibly be one of the most important presentations of her career.

'How on earth do you know that?' she asked abstractedly, and hoped her cheeks weren't bright red with embarrassment.

'Mel in Accounts told me.' Carolyn seemed blithely unaware of her discomfort.

Not for the first time Lucy felt as if she was working in a giant goldfish bowl. 'Well, it's just a bit of fun.' She shot a look around the busy department to see if any curious eyes were flicking her way. But thankfully it was Friday afternoon and everyone was at the far end of the office, all eyes and ears on computer screens and telephones, so that they could make a fast exit at five-thirty.

'It's about time you started to have some fun,' Carolyn continued unabashed. 'You've been working too hard recently.'

'Well, I suppose we all have. This takeover by EC Cruises has made us all worry about our jobs.'

'You're not kidding. I've hardly slept since the announcement last month and I'm not even in management.'

'I'm sure we will all feel better next week when the new owners come in to talk with us. Maybe there won't be any redundancies and things will tick along the same as before.'

'That's not what they are saying on the grapevine,' Carolyn muttered. 'They say EC Cruises are ruthless; they gobble up their competition and tear them apart.'

Lucy had heard that too. She had read up on the company last month and the facts hadn't been pleasant. 'No use worrying about that now,' she said firmly, trying not to think about it. 'We have other things to concentrate on at the moment.'

She glanced up and noticed that the MD and some of the members of the board were making their way down the corridor towards the boardroom. Carolyn was right: she had been working relentlessly hard. She had put months of preparation into her report for this afternoon. She just hoped it all hadn't been a waste of time now that the company had been taken over.

'I wish I was able to block things out the way you can, Lucy. You are always so cool and confident in a crisis.'

'Do you think so?' Lucy shook her head. There had been times when she had felt anything but cool and confident.

'Definitely. For example every time I look at that rat of an ex-husband of yours, I marvel that you are able to stand seeing him here every day in the office.'

'I've just come to terms with it.'

'You were always too good for him,' Carolyn continued dryly.

'Thanks for the vote of confidence, Caro.' Lucy smiled at her friend and closed her briefcase. Would she ever get away from the spectre of her ex-husband? she wondered.

As she glanced up through the glass partition she saw the object of her thoughts heading down the corridor. Kris was six years older than her, thirty-five now, and still a good-looking man if you liked blue-eyed men with blond hair. Personally, Lucy was completely off that type…in fact she was completely off men at the moment.

It was only the fact that her friend Mel wouldn't take no for an answer that was making her go speed dating tonight.

'You only have to give each man three minutes,' she had said coaxingly. 'And if you don't like any of them you go home and you don't need to see them again.' It sounded good in theory. Three minutes was about all the time she wanted to give to any man anyway.

Kris wasn't on his own, she noticed now. Another man had walked down the corridor to join him. He was taller than Kris, and broader. Lucy had always thought Kris had a good physique, but next to this guy he looked a bit weedy. In fact next to this guy he seemed to almost pale into insignificance.

Who was he? she wondered. As she stared at him he turned and their eyes met through the glass partition. He was very attractive: dark intense eyes, dark hair and a square jaw. He looked Spanish or maybe Latin American. He smiled at her and she gave a brief smile back and then hastily looked away.

The one thing she didn't need was complications at work. She had enough of those.

As if to prove the point, Carolyn was still going on about her ex-husband and how he'd probably regret what he'd done one day.

'Carolyn!' Lucy cut across her swiftly. 'If you don't mind I really don't want to talk about this…especially in *here*.' Lucy shot another look around the room. Whoever had designed open-plan offices should be taken out and shot, she thought forcefully.

Carolyn followed her gaze and grimaced. 'Sorry.' She mouthed the word. 'I'll ring you later.'

'Yes, good idea.'

Lucy put the letter she had brought her onto a spike with more force than was necessary. Carolyn was a nice person and a good friend, but she did go on too much. And Lucy was tired of being the focus of gossip. Surely people should be getting tired of discussing her marriage breakup by now?

One thing was for sure: she would never, *ever* date anyone at work again. Not that Kris had worked here when she had started dating him. That was another galling fact. She had been the one who had helped him get a job here.

Concentrate on work, she told herself fiercely. Kris and his blonde bombshell were welcome to each other. Holding her head high, Lucy picked up her briefcase and headed for the boardroom.

She was wearing a pinstriped dark trouser suit with a plain white blouse. Her long dark straight hair was caught back from her face. A few men looked over at her with interest as she took her place at the polished table, but she was unaware of their admiring glances. She was too busy getting out papers, going over last-minute figures in her mind.

Kris stepped in through the door behind her. 'Ah, Lucy, there you are,' he said briskly, as if she had been hiding in some dark corner of the universe. 'Mr Connors, I'd like you to meet the head of our marketing department, Lucy Blake. Lucy, this is Mr Connors who is visiting us from the new company headquarters in Barbados.'

Getting to her feet, Lucy found herself face to face with the man who had smiled at her in the corridor and a very strange thing happened. Everything flew out of her mind and she found herself forgetting how annoying Kris was, forgetting even where she was…and instead drowning in the most incredibly sexy dark-eyed gaze she had ever met.

'Pleased to meet you, Mr Connors.' She hadn't imagined it earlier—this man was simply gorgeous. Lucy was quite tall and there weren't many men who could make her feel petite, but he was one. He had to be well over six feet. His hair was thick and dark with a slight wave and his features were somehow powerfully arresting.

He smiled back at her and she noticed that his lips seemed to have a dominant curve that hinted at a strong sensuality.

What would it be like to be kissed by such a man? she

wondered hazily. To be taken into his arms and…well, just taken? Her stomach gave a wild flip of emotion.

Horrified, she unhooked her eyes from his. Never in her life had such a strange frisson of awareness shot through her. Maybe she had been on her own for too long, she thought wildly. To make up for it she put on her best, brisk, businesslike tone. 'Welcome to the London office.' She held out her hand.

'Thank you.' He looked as if her crisp formality amused him. But he enveloped her hand in a firm grip. 'And please call me Rick.'

Lucy didn't allow her hand to rest in his for a minute longer than was absolutely necessary. Somehow the touch of his skin against hers was deeply unsettling. But she inclined her head and murmured, 'Rick,' in acquiescence. Even the sound of his name on her lips seemed dangerously provocative somehow.

There was a moment's silence as she just stared up at him.

'Mr Connors is here to evaluate the way things are run in London.' Kris cut into the silence. 'He'll be with us for about a week and during that time it would be appreciated if you would give him every assistance, by answering his questions and taking time to show him exactly how your department works and has contributed towards making us one of the most successful cruising lines in the business.'

Why did Kris sound as if he'd just swallowed one of her brochures? Lucy wondered irately. She glanced up at him and he gave her a warm look of approval. Totally false, of course, Lucy reminded herself.

'Certainly.' Lucy steeled herself to look at Rick Connors again.

He smiled at her. 'Well, that's the gist of things, but we can be a little less formal about it.'

Was he Spanish American? she wondered. With dark,

smouldering looks like that she would have thought so, yet his name wasn't Spanish and his deep attractive tone was more mid-Atlantic, making it hard to place where he was from.

The MD, John Layton, came over to speak to them. 'Good to see you again, Rick.' The two men shook hands. 'I see you've met Lucy. She is an invaluable member of the team...invaluable. And she is going to kick things off for us today with a presentation on this season's forthcoming cruises.'

'Yes, so I believe, and I'm looking forward to it,' Rick drawled. Something about the way he said that, the way he looked at her, made an extra flutter of nerves stir in her stomach.

As the men moved away to talk to other members of the board Lucy gave a last-minute flick through her papers. She had prepared thoroughly for this and it was going to be no problem, she told herself calmly.

'Who is that handsome man?' her secretary Gina whispered as she slipped into the seat beside her. Lucy followed her gaze and smiled.

'Mr Connors, over from the new company in Barbados to check us out,' she told her succinctly. 'A sort of spy, I gather, possibly wanting to make sure we are all doing our jobs properly before the new bosses arrive next week.'

'He can check me out any time!' Gina breathed shakily. 'Talk about drop-dead gorgeous!'

'Probably married with three children,' Lucy murmured dismissively.

'Probably...' Gina still sounded dreamy. 'Which reminds me, have you heard the gossip?'

'What about?' Lucy asked, flicking through the slides she was going to show. 'Did you get me that file I asked for?'

'Yes, sorry it took me a while. I got sidetracked. I met

someone down the corridor who told me a bit of startling news.'

Lucy glanced at the papers she had passed over. 'What news?'

Her secretary hesitated:

The meeting was being called to order.

'For heaven's sake, Gina, spit it out,' Lucy murmured.

Her secretary leaned a little closer. 'Apparently your ex-husband's girlfriend is pregnant. Someone saw her; she's at least seven months.'

Lucy felt suddenly sick inside. It was crazy to feel like this, she told herself fiercely. Her marriage was over. She didn't care.

The MD was speaking. Then suddenly a hush had fallen over the room.

'Lucy?'

She was vaguely aware that everyone was looking at her, waiting for her to start her presentation.

Hastily she got to her feet. For a second her mind went completely blank. She glanced down the table and her eyes met with Kris's.

The sick feeling intensified inside her.

Kris seemed to be watching her very closely, possibly thinking that she was going to make a complete mess of this. The thought made her very quickly pull herself together.

'I am putting before you the proposed cruises for the forthcoming season...' She glanced down at her notes and then up again as she launched into the details. Her voice was clear and confident, her manner very businesslike.

Watching her, Rick was impressed. He liked the way she held the room spellbound. He liked her efficiency, her calm delivery. She had certainly done her homework. He watched as she flicked through the PowerPoint slides. The husky softness of her voice filled the darkened room.

There was something about her that really intrigued him. Maybe it was that flicker of vulnerability beneath the crisp confidence of her tone…or maybe it was just the fact that there was a very sexy body hiding beneath that crisp, businesslike suit.

The lights went back on and she was now inviting questions from the room. She glanced around the table and for a moment their eyes met, then quickly she looked away.

A couple of people asked her in-depth questions on cost analysis. She answered without hesitation.

Then the meeting moved on to wider aspects. John Layton spoke, and one of the accountants. Finally it was all over. As people packed their papers away and filed out of the room, Rick made his way towards her.

She glanced up at him and he noticed again that flicker of vulnerability in her eyes.

'Great presentation,' he said easily.

'Thanks.' She smiled briefly at him and then continued putting papers away.

'There was just one thing I wanted to ask you.'

'Yes?'

She looked up again and he watched the way she tucked a stray strand of hair behind her ear. He could almost see her mind ticking over, going through the facts and figures of her work.

'Would you like to have dinner with me tonight?'

He could see that he had definitely taken her by surprise.

Then quickly she looked away from him. 'Sorry, I can't tonight. I'm busy.'

Her tone was brisk.

'How about tomorrow, then?' Rick wasn't one for giving up easily.

'I can't tomorrow either.' She finished putting her papers away and snapped her briefcase shut before looking back up at him. 'Thank you for the invitation,' she said politely.

'But I never mix pleasure with business. It's a bad combination.'

Rick watched as she walked away and a smile touched his lips. It was years since he'd been turned down with such brisk resolve and he found it a very refreshing challenge. He liked her spirit—it intrigued him.

CHAPTER TWO

RICK glanced up from his newspaper as a waitress put down his drink.

'Bourbon on the rocks, Mr Connors,' she said with a smile.

'Thank you, Stacie,' he said, reading her name badge.

She smiled again and walked away. Rick folded his copy of the *Financial Times* and lifted his drink. His gaze drifted around the comfortable lounge with its pale gold flock sofas, down towards the hotel foyer. There was no doubt about it, Cleary's was a very stylish hotel, well deserving its five stars. He liked the high ceilings with their elaborate covings and chandeliers. He liked the polished wooden floors and the pale Egyptian rugs and the fact that real fires burned in the period fireplaces. Of all the hotels he owned around the world, this was undoubtedly one of his favourites. The place had a timeless elegance.

His gaze moved from the warmth of the interior out towards the window. Kensington looked bleak; rain was slanting almost sideways as bitter gusts of wind swept down the dark streets. He'd forgotten how much he disliked London in January. The place was abysmal. The sooner he got his business transactions completed and headed back to his house in Barbados, the better.

A black taxi pulled up outside and the hotel doorman stepped out to open the passenger door. Two women emerged. Rick sipped his drink and watched as the wind swooped on them, making one hold onto her black beret whilst her blonde hair swirled around her face. The other held onto her beige coat as it ruffled up showing a little glimpse of long, shapely legs in sheer stockings. They were both laughing breathlessly as they hurried towards the door.

'Whose mad idea was this?' the blonde asked as they stepped into the foyer. She took off her coat revealing a black dress that did little to disguise a curvaceous figure. But it was the brunette who held Rick's attention. He'd recognised her as soon as she had stepped out of the taxi. There was no mistaking that glorious tumbling dark hair and pale skin. What was Lucy doing at Cleary's? he wondered, intrigued.

'Actually, it was your mad idea,' she said, laughing over at her friend. 'And I don't know why I let you talk me into it. Any sane, sensible person would be tucked up at home with a bottle of wine and a roaring fire.'

'Yes, well, since when have you been sane and sensible? Come on, let's go get a glass of wine and eye up the talent.'

'Talent! Gosh, you're optimistic.'

'You may mock, but George Clooney could be waiting for me just at the other end of this corridor.'

'I think the only male likely to be out on a night like this is Donald Duck.'

They both laughed again.

Rick smiled to himself as he watched them walk down past the reception. Their voices and their laughter faded and silence descended again, a silence that seemed somehow less tranquil than before, somehow rather dull, in fact. Rick finished his drink and got up as curiosity got the better of him.

His feet sank into the luxurious rugs as he crossed towards the reception area.

'Evening, Mr Connors.' The head receptionist smiled at him as he wandered past.

'Evening.' He noticed a sign with an arrow pointing towards one of the banqueting suites that said, 'Speed dating located in the Mayfair Suite.'

'Speed dating?' One dark eyebrow lifted wryly as he looked back at the receptionist. 'Since when have we hosted speed dating events?'

'This is the first one.'

'Really—and whose idea was that?'

'That would be Julie Banks, our functions manager. Shall I get her for you? She is still on duty.'

'No, that won't be necessary, thank you.' Rick moved away from the reception and followed the arrows for the Mayfair Suite, down the long corridors.

The double doors to the suite were open. There were a lot of people milling around and tables and chairs had been set out on the ballroom floor. Rick's eyes flicked around the room and then spied Lucy sitting on one of the bar stools at the far end of the room.

Her coat had been dispensed with and she was wearing a pale blue Angora sweater with a sweetheart neckline, teamed with a pale blue skirt. As she swivelled sideways on the chair to glance around the room his gaze flicked downwards over her shapely legs to her high heels in two-tone blue and beige. There was something very classy about Lucy Blake, almost preppy, he thought.

The woman organising the event was standing a few yards away giving instructions to a member of staff. She was middle-aged, wearing dark-rimmed glasses and a smart black suit that sat rather awkwardly on her very thin frame. However, there was nothing awkward about her manner, which was brisk and efficient, and there was no doubting who was in charge.

As Rick made to go across to her the functions manager hurtled in through the door behind him and waylaid him. 'Mr Connors, they told me you were looking for me at Reception,' she said breathlessly and thrust out her hand. 'I'm Julie Banks, Functions Manager. Is there anything wrong? Can I help you?'

'Not at all, Julie, I'm just being nosy.' He smiled reassuringly at the harassed-looking blonde. 'I just wondered what kind of response you'd had to this speed-dating idea.'

She visibly seemed to relax. 'Well, as you can see we've had a big response. I thought we'd just try it out—we've been thinking of ways to fill up the third function suite at off-peak periods. We had an arts and crafts seminar last week and that was successful as well, but—'

'If you'll excuse me, Julie, I just want to speak to the lady organising things for a moment.'

'Oh, but she isn't employed by the hotel, she just runs these speed-dating events at different places—'

'Yes, that's fine, Julie.' Rick moved purposefully away from the woman, but she trailed after him, an anxious look stretched across her young face.

The organiser was ruffling through pages of paper on a clipboard as Rick approached.

'Yes, your name, please?' she asked abruptly without looking up.

'Rick Connors.'

'C…for Connors…you don't seem to be down here. Have you paid your fee, Mr Connors?' Still she didn't look up.

Julie Banks started to edge in nervously. 'Em…you don't quite understand, Ms Sullivan. Er, Mr Connors is—'

'It doesn't matter who he is, Ms Banks. If his name isn't on the list he can't take part in the speed dating.' She darted a rather frosty glance at the functions manager.

'*Mr Connors* doesn't want to take part.' Julie sounded horrified. 'You don't understand… I should introduce you properly. Mr Connors is the owner of this hotel and—'

'I just want to take part fleetingly.' Rick cut in smoothly and was amused momentarily by the fact that Julie's mouth had dropped open. 'Five minutes at the end of proceedings will do me. I just want to speak to one particular woman.'

'But that's not how it works, Mr Connors.' For the first

time Ms Sullivan looked at Rick and her voice altered immediately to a softer more encouraging tone. 'You see, the idea is that you spend a few minutes with each person and that way you can gauge which woman you'd like to see again. Then you tick her name in the box on your sheet and if she also ticks your name, you have a match.'

'Yes, but I already know which woman I'd like to see again. So I'd like to skip the preliminaries.' Rick reached into his inside pocket and took out a wallet. 'And I'm willing to pay, of course.'

Ms Sullivan looked flustered now. 'Well, this is highly irregular.'

Rick smiled at her. 'I know. But I thought it might be a bit of fun. So perhaps you'd be kind enough to bend the rules just this once…'

Ms Sullivan pushed her glasses further up her nose. 'Well, I…suppose I could.'

'This is really very kind of you, Ms Sullivan. Most appreciated.'

'I told you there would be a lot of people here,' Mel said smugly.

'Yes, you were right,' Lucy remarked, but her attention was on her new shoes. She should never have worn them tonight; they were too high and her feet were killing her already.

'This is the modern way to meet people. It's just perfect for busy career girls like us. One night and approximately thirty dates—what more could a girl ask for?'

'Hmm…' Lucy took another sip of her drink. 'Let me see now. Hot bath? Good book? Both sound like heaven to me.'

'Oh, that's rubbish! You're just scared of getting involved with someone again.'

For some reason a picture of Rick Connors asking her out to dinner flashed in her mind. If he hadn't been involved with the company she knew she would have been tempted to go out with him. 'I'm not scared of anything!' Lucy said hotly. 'And I have been out on a few dates since Kris and I divorced, so you can't accuse me of living life like a nun.'

'A few dates that led to you being back in your flat and tucked up in your bed by ten with a mug of cocoa,' Mel said scathingly.

'Well, I didn't really fancy any of them.' Lucy scowled at her. 'And I couldn't get involved with someone if I really didn't fancy them…if there was no spark.'

'So what about that Ryan guy? He was very good-looking. Why didn't you fancy him?' Mel persisted.

Lucy shrugged. 'Well, for a start he lied to me, told me he'd never been married, then halfway through dinner he admitted that he was divorced and that he'd left his wife. It put me off him.'

'For heaven's sake, Luce, if you're looking for the perfect man then you're never going to find him. Such a creature doesn't exist.'

'Yes, but you know how I feel about lies. I had a bellyful of them when I was married to Kris. I don't want a man who can't be truthful.'

'Maybe he was just too upset to talk about his divorce.'

'Maybe,' Lucy conceded.

'Anyway, I think you are approaching this man thing with the wrong mindset.'

'How do you mean?' Lucy took a sip of her wine.

'Well, you don't want to get married again just yet, do you?'

'No!' Lucy shook her head.

'Or live with anyone?'

'I want my independence,' Lucy said firmly. 'It will be a long time before I do anything like that again…if ever.' But for a moment she thought about the fact that she had wanted a baby… She hadn't told Mel about Kris's girlfriend being pregnant. Somehow it hurt too much to talk about.

She swallowed hard and tried not to think about it.

'You need to view relationships and men in a different light—follow a whole different set of criteria,' Mel continued.

'Yes, you're right.'

'You're looking for a man who sets your pulses on fire—nothing else. It doesn't matter if he's not the settling-down type. Because all you want is a no-strings, sophisticated affair. And, believe me, there is *nothing* as exciting as one of those. You tumble into bed and have wild, passionate sex and meet for secret assignations…and real life never has to cloud things. Then when the novelty wears off you move on to the next conquest.'

'I don't think I'm ready for that, Mel,' Lucy said lightly. To be honest she didn't know if she would ever be ready for that. It all sounded a bit too modern for her. 'I don't think it's quite my thing.'

'Listen; after all you've been through you need a little light fun,' Mel insisted firmly.

'Yes, I agree with that. But just a little light flirtation will do for now.' Lucy swirled her wine around in her glass and tried to work up some enthusiasm for the evening. 'So what's the talent like out there?' She took another sip of her wine. 'Have you seen George Clooney yet?'

'Actually, there's an absolutely gorgeous man talking to the woman who is organising things. Move over, George. I can't wait to have my three minutes with him, I can tell you.'

Lucy swivelled around in her chair and searched the crowd. 'Where? I can't see him.'

'He was there a moment ago.' Mel frowned. 'Damn. Well, anyway, just remember I bagged him first.'

'Okay, I'll remember.' Lucy grinned.

The organiser was calling everyone to the tables and chairs on the dance floor so there was no further time for conversation.

Immediately Lucy sat down, a man sat opposite her and the dating game began. Surprisingly, after the first few men Lucy started to relax and enjoy herself. It was quite good fun being chatted up by someone new every few minutes; there wasn't time to feel awkward, and on the whole she had a laugh with each person who sat opposite. In fact time seemed to fly past.

None of the men set her pulses racing, though there was one, a Mark Kirkland, who was semi interesting and not bad-looking. She made a note of him on the form she had been given and ticked his name in the box.

'So what's a nice girl like you doing in a place like this?' A deep sexy voice interrupted her writing.

'That's not a very original line, if I may say so...' She glanced up with a smile and met Rick Connors' dark, steady gaze.

CHAPTER THREE

'WHAT on earth are you doing here?' A wave of surprise rippled through Lucy's entire body...along with some other inexplicable emotion that was very disturbing.

'You just told me that was a very unoriginal question,' Rick reminded her with a grin.

'Yes...but...' Her brain seemed to have gone into free fall, along with her stomach. '*Really*, what are you doing here?' she repeated distractedly.

'Actually, I'm staying here at this hotel.'

'The company have put you up at Cleary's!'

He watched the incredulous expression on her face with a grin. 'You find that hard to believe?'

'Well...yes. It must cost a fortune to stay here. EC Cruises must be very generous with their staff.'

'They try to look after them.' He grinned.

'Well, that's good news,' Lucy said lightly. 'Maybe they'll do something about the drinks machine at the office.'

'Is it bad?'

Lucy raised an eyebrow. 'Have you tasted the coffee from it, and seen how much they charge us for it?'

Rick grinned. 'No, but thanks for the warning. I'll put it on my list of recommended changes.'

She wanted to ask him if that was his job in the company, recommending changes, but maybe this wasn't the time or the place. 'So have the company really installed you here for the whole week?' she asked lightly instead.

For a moment Rick hesitated and contemplated telling her the truth: that he wasn't an employee of EC Cruises, that he owned the company and Cleary's was one of a family of hotels also owned by him. He opened his mouth and then as he met the candid green beauty of her eyes closed it again. He liked the way Lucy acted around him, liked the fact that unlike other people she didn't fawn over his every word. Her naturalness was a refreshing change in a world where everyone was impressed by his power and wealth. And, besides, he was in London to inspect his new acquisition from the grass roots up. He didn't want anyone at the office knowing who he was yet; it would make it harder to really assess things. The only person to know his true identity was John Layton.

'Well, actually EC Cruises own this hotel,' he said instead with a shrug. 'So they've found me a broom cupboard for the week.'

'That figures.' Lucy smiled at him. 'So have you tried speed dating before?'

'No, this is all new to me. As a matter of fact I saw you arrive and just followed you through.' He grinned. 'I was curious as to why you turned my dinner invitation down.'

'My secret is out.' Lucy smiled. 'I had a previous engagement with thirty men.'

'Do you go speed dating often?'

'No.' Lucy shook her head. 'To be honest I've been dragged here by a friend. It's a whole new experience.'

'And what do you think of it?'

Her eyes drifted over him. What she was thinking at the moment was how exceptionally handsome he was. She noticed how expensive his suit looked, how easily it sat on his broad shoulders, how his crisp white shirt was open at the neck revealing a healthy tan. His dark hair seemed to glint under the overhead chandeliers and he really had the most incredibly sexy eyes, eyes that seemed to be burning into hers.

Realising he was waiting for her to answer him, she hurriedly gathered her senses. 'I think it's been good fun.'

'Well, I'm certainly glad I wandered in,' he murmured. There was a seductive tone to his voice now that, teamed with the way he was watching her, made her feel even hotter inside. 'And it's given me a real insight into the London office.'

Lucy was relieved that he had lightened his tone, was glad to be able to joke back. 'Well, if this is all part of your work assessment for the company, then I think you might be going above and beyond the call of duty.'

'I'm getting a generous overtime rate, so what the heck?' He shrugged and his lips twisted in a ruggedly attractive smile. 'So tell me, have you ticked many names on that form yet?' He nodded at the piece of paper in front of her.

Lucy hesitated and then decided to play along. 'Just one. What about you?'

'Just one.' His eyes held hers.

With difficulty she wrenched her gaze away. 'Actually I can't see your name on this list,' she told him quickly as she looked back down at the form in front of her.

'That's because it's not there. I was too late a contender, but don't worry, the indomitable Ms Sullivan said it was all right. You can just pencil me in at the bottom of the page.' He grinned at her wryly. 'Or better still, we could dispense with the formalities. How about joining me for a drink in the bar?'

The suddenly serious question took her by surprise. 'Well…when were you thinking?'

'Now.' He grinned at her. 'After all, there's no time like the present. And I bet you're thirsty after all the talking you've been doing.'

Danger signals started to course through her in thunderous waves. This man was just too attractive…and he was having too weird an effect on her senses. Suddenly it felt safer to start backing away from the situation. 'Thanks for the offer, Rick. But I don't think it's a good idea.'

'Why not?' He didn't seem in the least thrown by her refusal.

'I told you earlier; I've made it a rule never to get involved with anyone at work.'

'Very sensible.' He nodded his head. 'But I don't think I count as someone at work. After all, I'm only going to be in the country for a week.'

'Yes, but even so, we will be working together on Monday, so—'

'All the more reason to get better acquainted before then.' He cut across her and leaned his elbows on the table, watching her with great amusement. 'I'm only suggesting we have a drink—jumping into bed together is optional.' He watched the flare of colour in her cheeks and his grin stretched wider. 'Sorry, am I embarrassing you?'

Embarrassment was far too light a word for what he was doing to her. For some reason her blood pressure seemed to have rocketed just at the mention of going to bed with him. 'No, of course not, and, I assure you, jumping into bed with you was the last thing on my mind.' With a supreme effort she managed to sound composed.

'Now, that's a shame,' he drawled, still with that note of warm enjoyment in his tone.

Lucy glanced away from him and noticed with relief that the speed dating had finished and that most people had stood up and were milling around chatting. She spied Mel standing a little further away, talking to the organiser.

'Well, I think things have come to an end here,' she said, pushing her chair back from the table. 'And I've arranged to share a cab back home with my friend, so I really should go.'

Rick also rose to his feet. She noticed again how tall he was, how petite he made her feel.

'Anyway, Rick, nice talking to you,' she said in what she hoped was a dismissive tone.

Before she could turn and walk away, however, Mel arrived beside them.

'Hi.' She flashed a brilliant smile at Rick, batting her wide blue eyes and tossing back her long blonde mane of hair. 'I think something went terribly wrong with the organisation on this event, because we didn't get to meet up. I'm Melanie Roberts.'

'Hi, Melanie.' Rick bestowed a very warm smile on her and took the hand that she offered. 'I'm Rick Connors. Lucy and I know each other from work.'

'Oh, I see! I work in the accounts office but I haven't seen you around.' Melanie darted a look of surprise over at Lucy, a look that clearly said: How come you haven't told me about this man?

'Rick is from the new head office in Barbados, here to assess operations,' Lucy explained. 'He only arrived today.'

'I haven't got around all the departments yet,' Rick said easily.

'Oh, I see.'

Mel was starting to sound like a parrot, Lucy thought with irritation. And did she have to look up at Rick with such adoring eyes? It was no wonder the guy was so coolly confident.

'I was just suggesting to Lucy that we head off for a drink in the bar. But she tells me that you are both dashing for a taxi,' Rick informed her lightly.

Mel darted a look at Lucy that said very clearly she thought she was mad. 'We don't have to dash off straight away, Lucy,' she said with scolding emphasis. 'I'm sure we've got time for one drink.'

Before Lucy could say anything to this Rick was taking control. 'Well, that's settled, then. Let's head for the bar, shall we?'

'Great idea.' Mel pointedly ignored the fact that Lucy was

glaring at her and linked her arm with Rick. 'So how long are you here for, Rick?' she asked jovially.

'Just a week.'

'And then it's back to Barbados, is it?'

'That's right.'

A member of staff came around collecting their forms. 'If you have a match you will be contacted via your e-mail or contact number,' Ms Sullivan informed everyone loudly.

Lucy handed hers in and then, faced with no other alternative, found herself trailing along beside Rick towards the bar.

'I'd love to go to Barbados.' Mel glanced across Rick's chest at Lucy. 'Luce would as well, wouldn't you, Luce?'

'Well, I—'

'In fact Lucy was only saying the other day how much she could do with some sunshine,' Mel continued merrily.

'You should take one of the cruises that you sell so well,' Rick said, looking over at Lucy.

'I fly out to Miami occasionally to inspect new ships.' Lucy shrugged. 'But there's never time to sit in the sun.'

Rick looked at her with a raised eyebrow. 'Now that is a definite oversight on the part of the company. How can you sell something when you have never tried it?'

'I have all the necessary details about the cruises at my fingertips,' Lucy said with another shrug. 'That's all I need.'

'Well, I'll grant that you certainly know your job,' Rick said easily. 'That much was very clear during your presentation today.'

The bar lounge had filled up, but they managed to find some seats in an alcove. Rick glanced around for a waitress, then decided he'd probably get served quicker at the bar. 'What can I get you to drink?' he asked them. 'How about a cocktail?'

They both ordered a Margarita.

'He's very handsome,' Mel said dreamily as they watched him weave his way through the crowds towards the bar.

'I suppose he is,' Lucy conceded. 'A bit pushy, though. I'd turned down the offer of a drink.'

'Yes, and it's a good job I was here to rescue the situation. Honestly, Luce, you don't turn down someone like him.'

'He's from work, and you know I have rules about that.'

'Then it's about time you threw that rule book of yours away,' Mel said firmly. 'But if you don't want him…well, hey, I had my eye on him first anyway.'

'Is he the guy you saw earlier?'

'Of course he is. How many men like him can you see floating around?' Mel grinned over at her. 'I'd say I'd fight you for him, but unfortunately he only seems to have eyes for you so I think I'd lose the battle.'

'Rubbish. He's over here on business and just at a loose end, that's all.'

'Maybe so, but he still fancies you. I can read the signs, which is why I'm going to make an excuse and leave in a few minutes.'

'Mel! You are to do no such thing!' Lucy said in alarm. Somehow the thought of being left alone with Rick Connors made her heart race with very peculiar panic.

'You *do* like him, don't you?' Mel's grin stretched wider. 'Well, good. It's about time you took a dive into a little romantic water. This could be just what you need to get you back in the flow.'

'Mel, you are not to leave…' Lucy insisted urgently, but there wasn't time to say anything else because Rick arrived back.

'So what shall we drink to?' he asked with a grin as he took a seat opposite Lucy and put the drinks on the table.

'How about speed dating?' Mel suggested.

'Speed dating it is,' Rick said as he raised his glass.

A waitress stopped by their table. 'Can I get you anything, Mr Connors?'

'No, we're fine, thanks.' Rick smiled up at her easily.

The woman smiled back at him warmly and fluttered her eyelashes a little. 'Well, anything else you need, don't hesitate to call me over.'

'The staff are very attentive in here, aren't they?' Mel murmured as the woman left them. 'And she remembered your name!'

'Yes, they certainly train their staff well. The personal touch is very important, don't you think?' Rick murmured.

Although she agreed with him, Lucy couldn't help but think that probably every woman with a pulse would remember Rick's name. And any woman who fell for Rick Connors would be asking for big trouble. He had heartbreaker written all over him in capital letters. She wondered if he had a wife or a girlfriend waiting patiently for him back in Barbados.

He looked across and met her eyes and smiled.

Silly question, she thought hazily. Some woman would definitely be waiting for him.

'That's my phone,' Mel said suddenly as she took her mobile out of her bag.

'I didn't hear anything.' Lucy looked over at her suspiciously.

'Well, it was. I've had a message.' Mel peered at the screen. 'Oh, dear, I'm afraid I'm going to have to leave. It's from my mother. I completely forgot that I said I'd call in on the way home and she's waiting patiently for me.' Mel popped the phone back in her bag. 'I am sorry about this.' She carefully avoided looking at Lucy, who was frowning at her, and smiled instead at Rick. 'It was lovely meeting you, Rick. Maybe we'll meet again before you return to Head Office.'

'I hope so, Mel.' He grinned at her. 'And it was good meeting you too.'

'And don't let this one—' she pointed at Lucy '—dash off home too early. Contrary to what she thinks, her clothes will not turn to rags when the clock strikes twelve.'

'Very funny, Mel,' Lucy said dryly.

With a mischievous grin Mel picked up her bag and walked away.

'So, alone at last,' Rick said with a smile as she looked across and met his dark steady gaze.

The teasing tone and the way he looked at her caused another flurry of disquiet inside Lucy. 'I don't know where Mel is dashing off to in such a hurry,' she murmured distractedly. 'Her mother moved to live in the South of France over a year ago.'

Rick laughed at that. 'Well, maybe she's suddenly remembered a hot date.'

'Maybe,' Lucy murmured. 'Or maybe she has the wrong impression about us...imagined that she was playing gooseberry or something stupid like that.'

Rick's gaze swept slowly over her. There was no doubt about it; Lucy was an extremely attractive woman. And the fact that every aspect of her body language was telling him clearly to keep his distance, from the tips of her beautifully shod feet to the way she held her head high, her chin angled up slightly, intrigued him immensely.

'Now, I wonder where she could have got a ludicrous idea like that from,' he said softly, a gleam of sardonic humour in his voice.

'Lord alone knows.' Lucy crossed her long legs and leaned back in her chair. 'I did try to tell her that we are just work colleagues, but I don't think she believed me.'

Rick's gaze was distracted for a moment by the way she crossed her legs, by the sensuous curves of her body held so ramrod straight in her chair.

Then as their eyes met again he noted that she was very aware of his scrutiny, and for a second there was a flicker of warmth in the wide beauty of her eyes that told very clearly she wasn't immune to him.

He smiled at her and watched the slight flush of colour in the smooth, high cheeks. Hastily she looked away from him.

'So, Rick, what are your impressions about our London office?' she asked as she took a sip of her drink.

He noted how swiftly she brought the subject of conversation round to work like a hastily erected barrier with a sign that stated very clearly that trespassers onto private property would be prosecuted. It wasn't the kind of reaction he was used to from a woman, and it amused him, aroused a feeling of challenge inside him.

'I think the London office has some very strong possibilities,' he drawled slowly.

'Possibilities?' She looked confused. 'How do you mean?'

'I mean there is room for development.'

'Is that a polite way of saying there is room for improvement?'

He laughed at that. 'Maybe. Isn't there always room for improvement with everything?'

'I suppose so. But John Layton runs a pretty tight ship, if you'll pardon the pun.'

Rick smiled. 'Yes, so I've been told. I've also been told that you have helped him a great deal. That in fact it was your marketing skills that facilitated a turn-around in the company's fortunes last year.'

'I wouldn't go that far,' Lucy said firmly. 'As you probably know, there was a slump in profits for a while last year, but things have picked up again and it's not just down to me. There has been an upswing in the economy, which has helped, plus we have good teamwork at the London office.'

'Modest as well as talented,' Rick remarked with a grin and watched the glow of colour in her cheeks. 'But I know how much your input has helped. I've read numerous reports on the upswing of the company's profit margins. And your name has cropped up several times when I've been talking to John.'

Lucy felt a little uncomfortable with the praise. 'Well, as I said before I have a good team working with me.' Her eyes narrowed on him for a moment as she noticed suddenly his easy use of the MD's first name.

'So what exactly is your job?' she asked curiously. 'How come you are reading past financial records? Are you employed by EC Cruises as a kind of troubleshooter?'

Rick thought about that for a moment. 'Yes, I suppose I am a troubleshooter of sorts. I look for ways of getting the best out of a business, of maximising profits.'

'And do you do that by cutting staff?' She probably shouldn't have asked that question, but she had read the reports about the company he worked for and she wasn't overly impressed.

'Not always, no,' he answered calmly. 'I make an assessment of every aspect of the business and I take it from there.'

Lucy nodded. She supposed he was just following orders, and doing his job. She couldn't dislike him for that.

'So you're an accountant?' She lifted her glass and took a sip.

'I trained as an economist and then branched out a little from there.'

For some reason she was glad that he wasn't an accountant. Kris was an accountant and she didn't want him to have anything in common with her ex. As the thought crossed her mind she frowned. It didn't matter what Rick did for a living because it was of no significance to her, and anyway wasn't there a bit of a fine line between accountant and economist?

'What about you? Have you always worked in marketing?'

Lucy shook her thoughts away from any comparisons with Kris. 'I've been with the company for four years, before that I worked for Galaxino, they're a big—'

'Advertising company,' he finished for her. 'Yes, I've heard of them.'

Lucy nodded. 'I got a bit bored with them, used to spend a lot of my days thinking up new ways to sell shampoo...'

'So are you happy working where you are?'

'Yes, I suppose I'm happy for now.' Lucy tried not to think about the gossip she would have to endure once it became public knowledge about Kris becoming a father. 'I'll have to wait and see what changes are made now we've been taken over,' she added briskly.

'There will be meetings next week to discuss all that.'

'Yes, I gather the big boss is coming.' Lucy swirled her drink around the glass. 'Do you know him well?'

'You could say that.' Rick smiled.

'Everyone has been very on edge about this takeover, you know.'

Rick nodded. 'It's a difficult time. But they have no need to be.'

'We'll have to wait and see, I suppose.' She looked over at him directly then. 'You'll have been involved in a lot of EC takeovers, I suppose.'

'A fair few over the years,' he agreed.

'Do you enjoy your job?'

'Yes, I do. I get to do a lot of travelling. We have offices in Miami and New York as well as Barbados and London.'

'And you live in Barbados?'

He nodded. 'What about you? Have you always lived in London?'

She looked over at him and smiled. 'No, I was brought up in Devon.'

'You're a country girl, then?'

She smiled. 'In my heart anyway.'

'You don't have an accent.'

'No…well, I moved to London when I was thirteen.' She took another sip of her drink. 'You don't have an accent either.'

'I moved around a lot when I was growing up. My father was Irish and my mother from Buenos Aires. My real name is Enrique, but everyone has always just called me Rick.'

That explained his Latin good looks, she thought idly, her gaze moving over the darkness of his hair and eyes. 'Do you speak Spanish?'

To her surprise he answered her in the language. It sounded warmly sensual and it had a perturbing effect on her senses. 'What does that mean?' she asked hesitantly.

'It means I'm very glad that we bumped into each other this evening.' He smiled and it had an even more disturbing effect.

'Would you like another drink?' he asked as the waitress passed close to their table.

'Actually, I'd better not have any more,' she said quickly. 'I don't really drink a lot and I've already had wine tonight.'

He didn't press her.

The bar was starting to empty now, Lucy noticed. She glanced at her watch and noticed it was almost eleven-thirty. 'Actually I didn't realise how late it was.' She looked over at him. 'I really ought to be going.'

It surprised her how much she regretted saying that; there was a part of her that could have sat on here and talked to him all night. She would have liked to know more about him.

Rick Connors was very interesting, she decided. She liked the warmth of his gaze, the humour in his tone…the way her body went hot all over when he looked at her in a certain way... The thought crept in surreptitiously catching her by surprise and sending a wave of renewed heat through her. It was a long time since a man had had that effect on her and it was truly disconcerting. Hastily she reached for her coat.

'Your clothes won't really turn to rags at midnight, you know,' Rick teased lightly.

'No, but my transport might disappear and that would be much worse. It can be hard getting a taxi when the weather is so bad.' She smiled back at him and as their eyes met she felt a shiver of sexual awareness slice straight through her. Hurriedly she turned away from him and stood up.

'I'll see you home,' Rick said, rising to his feet with her.

'Oh, no, really, there's no need.' She looked up at him, flustered by the offer. 'I'll just take a taxi from outside.'

'Well, I'll come and see you safely into your taxi, then.'

Lucy tried to protest, but he had hold of her arm and was walking with her towards the front entrance.

'It's still raining,' Lucy noticed as they neared the glass doors and saw the rain slanting down onto the road in diagonal sheets. 'Don't come outside, Rick.'

But he ignored her and as the doorman opened the ornate door for them he stepped out under the awning into the bitter cold air with her.

'Good night, Mr Connors.' The doorman touched his hat.

'How does he know your name?' Lucy asked, perplexed.

'I was talking to him earlier.' Rick glanced along the pavement. They weren't the only ones standing under the hotel's wide awning waiting for a taxi; there was a crowd of people in front of them. 'You know, it might be quicker to go back inside and ring for a taxi...in fact, this hotel has a fleet of limousines. We could ring for one of them.'

'Are you joking?' Lucy looked up at him in astonishment. 'That would cost a fortune.'

'Would it?' Rick shrugged. 'I could always put it on expenses,' he suggested with a grin.

She laughed at that. 'Yes, I suppose you could if you don't mind losing your job.'

For a moment Rick contemplated telling her the truth: that it wouldn't cost him anything, that he owned the hotel and the limousines and the phenomenally high expense account was his to do with as he pleased. But then she might start acting differently around him…and, well…this was fun. So instead he said lightly, 'At least come back inside so I can ring for a taxi. This weather is horrendous.'

Lucy watched the way the rain was bouncing off the pavements. 'I won't melt. I'm made of tougher stuff. Actually there's a tube station not far from here, I might head up there… Oh, hold on.' She broke off as a red double-decker bus rounded the corner. 'I can catch this. It goes right to the bottom of my road.'

'A bus! Hang on, Lucy, you'd be better getting a taxi at this time of night.'

'No need, honestly. I'll be fine.' She was pulling up the collar on her coat as she spoke. 'Thanks for the drink, Rick.'

The next moment she was gone, darting out into the rain and dashing towards the bus stop.

Rick hesitated for just a second and then set off after her.

CHAPTER FOUR

LUCY only just caught the bus and was slightly out of breath as she got on board. Downstairs was packed so she climbed the stairs and found herself alone up there.

She sat down and stared out of the dark, rain-streaked windows as the bus rattled off down the road again, and for a moment she thought back on the evening and the peculiar effect Rick had on her senses. There had been a part of her that had been glad to run away from him…and another that couldn't help regretting the fact that he hadn't kissed her. If she'd hung around would that have happened? And what would it have felt like? Maybe she had been imagining it, but there had seemed to be a very strong chemistry between them.

Someone slid into the seat beside her and she looked round in alarm, wondering why anyone would sit so close when there were so many empty seats. She didn't know if she was relieved or not as she met Rick's dark gaze because her heart seemed to do an almost violent somersault. 'What on earth are you doing here?'

'That's the second time you've asked me that tonight.' He looked amused. 'The fact is, I couldn't let you travel home alone at night on a bus. I mean, anything could happen to you.'

For a moment her lips curved in a wry smile. 'This is London, Rick. Not Miami.'

'Actually Miami is pretty safe these days,' Rick countered. 'But, call me old-fashioned, I just wanted to see you safely to your front door.'

There was something about the sincerity of his tone that

touched her. Since Kris had left she'd had to get used to looking out for herself. No one had worried about whether she got home safely in a very long time.

'That's very kind of you…but there was no need,' she added hastily. 'Actually I have a black belt in karate, so I can look after myself, you know.'

'Really?' He watched as she pushed her wet hair back from her face, noticing how small and slender her wrists were. She didn't look as if she could fend off a fly, never mind a strong attacker.

'Yes, really.' Her green eyes glittered with a sudden boldness and she angled her chin up defiantly. 'Don't you believe me?'

Her slender femininity gave him a cause not to, yet the determination in her eyes, in her demeanour, made him think again. 'Yes, I believe you,' he said with a grin.

'Good.' She grinned back at him. 'I'd have hated it if I'd had to throw you to the ground just to prove my point.'

One dark eyebrow rose slightly. 'Oh, I don't know…' he murmured with teasing seductiveness. 'I might have liked falling at your feet. It sounds kind of promising.'

For some reason the tone of his voice, the gleam of his eye made her pulses race, made her blush.

She looked away from him. 'Anyway, it is very gallant of you to see me home. I'll have to buy you a coffee in the office as a thank-you.'

'Okay, I'll hold you to that,' he said firmly. 'But after what you've told me about the coffee in the office I'm going to insist we go out.'

'If we have time,' Lucy countered. 'It can be pretty hectic in that office on a Monday.'

'Don't worry, we'll find some time to play truant,' he assured her solemnly.

'I thought you were being employed by the company to

try and make things better in the office, not worse,' she said with a smile.

'I've been given a pretty wide remit,' he assured her. 'Lunch can go under the heading of getting to know the staff and their requirements.'

'Lunch! We were talking about coffee.' She laughed and then said jokingly, 'And it had better be all above board, because I'm very conscientious, you know. And you can pass that message on to the new boss.'

'Don't worry, I will.' He smiled at her. 'You have some very admirable qualities, Ms Blake.'

His voice had a husky, very sexy quality and he seemed to be looking very deeply into her eyes. She noticed how dark his eyes were, noticed the golden flecks in their depths. His skin was a smooth olive colour and there was the beginning of a dark shadow along the square lines of his jaw. For a moment her eyes lingered on the sensual curve of his lips and she felt her heart starting to pound against her chest with the painful awareness that she would give anything for him to kiss her. He was just too…gorgeous.

Realising suddenly that they were just sitting there staring at each other, she pulled her gaze away and glanced out of the window. 'I think we're nearing my stop.' Her voice wobbled peculiarly and she frowned, hating herself for allowing her emotions to take over from common sense. He was a work colleague, she told herself fiercely, and her number one rule was not to get involved with anyone from work. 'Yes, it is my stop,' she added with relief. 'We need to get off here.'

Rick slid out from the seat and preceded her down the stairs. Then as she stepped off the bus he held out his hand to help her.

'Thanks.' Her hand rested in his for a moment and then hastily she pulled away.

The rain had abated a little, but it was still drizzling and cold. Lucy huddled further into her coat and glanced up at Rick. 'How are you planning to get back to the hotel?' she asked suddenly.

'I'll think about that when I've seen you to your front door. Which way is it?'

She was going to argue that there was no need for him to come any further, but it seemed churlish as he had already come this far. 'It's just around the corner.'

They set off walking. It was very quiet, just an occasional car swishing along the waterlogged roads past them. As they turned into the elegant Georgian square where Lucy had her apartment the rain started to come down in earnest.

'Maybe you should turn back now.' Lucy gasped as the icy water lashed against them.

'As you said earlier, I won't melt.' Rick reached out and caught hold of her hand. 'Come on, we'd better hurry.'

After a moment's hesitation she was running along beside him, jumping over puddles on the pavement. This was the second time tonight he had taken hold of her hand and she liked it, liked the fact that they were both laughing breathlessly by the time they arrived outside her house.

'Nice area,' Rick remarked as he let go of her and looked up at the buildings that curved so gracefully around the small park in the centre.

'Yes, I like it. Let's get out of this rain.' Lucy led the way up the steps so that they could stand in the shelter of the vestibule.

'It was very kind of you to see me home.' She turned to look up at him.

'It was no problem.' He stepped a little closer and for some reason her heart started to thump wildly against her chest. This was crazy, but she felt like a teenager on a first date.

She looked past him back at the street. 'The rain seems to be easing a bit now. There's a tube station on the road where the bus dropped us. Just turn left up there.' She waved airily back in the direction they had come from. 'It might be quicker than waiting for a bus or a taxi.'

He nodded.

Her eyes drifted over his broad shouldered frame. He wasn't wearing a coat and the expensive suit shimmered with raindrops in the light that slanted out from the hallway. 'Perhaps you had better come in and dry off before heading back?' The words were out of her mouth before she could stop them.

He didn't answer immediately.

'Unless you'd rather not.' Hurriedly she tried to back-track. 'I suppose it is rather late.'

'Not that late.' He smiled at her. 'And I'd love to come in, thanks.'

His smile did funny things to her pulse rate, made it skip unevenly. Nervously she searched in her bag for her front-door key.

Lucy was very aware of his eyes on her as she walked in front of him across the wide hallway and up the graceful curving staircase. 'I live up on the second floor so it's quite a climb, I'm afraid.'

'That must be what keeps you so beautifully slim,' he remarked.

It was just a light-hearted remark, but it caused the but-terflies in her stomach to flutter even more.

Lucy fitted the key in her front-door lock and wondered suddenly if she had left the place tidy. She had been in such a rush trying to get ready to go out that she hadn't had time to do much in the way of housework. And she had certainly never imagined in her wildest dreams that she would bring anyone home with her.

It was a relief to find the place didn't look too bad. The cushions on the settee were a bit higgledy-piggledy and there were a few newspapers and magazines on the glass coffee-table, but it could have been worse.

'Sorry about the mess,' she said as she took off her coat and hastily rearranged the cushions and gathered up the papers.

Rick watched her, a gleam of amusement in his dark eyes. 'I think you are a bit of a perfectionist, Lucy.'

'No, not really. To be honest I've been so busy at work recently that I haven't had a lot of time for housework.'

His gaze moved around the room. It had a comfortable elegance with its maple floor and the wide bay windows that no doubt would look out over the park. Her décor was pleasing on the eye. Everything was plain; the only colour was the vibrant pictures on the walls and the books that were crammed into bookshelves along one side of the room.

Lucy moved to light the fire. 'I bet you're missing the heat of Barbados.'

'You're not kidding. I'd forgotten how cold London can be.'

'At least the gale-force wind has dropped. When Mel and I arrived at Cleary's tonight we were nearly blown away.'

'I know. I saw you.' Rick grinned.

Lucy looked over at him in surprise.

'I was sitting in the front lounge.' Rick moved to look at some of the pictures on the walls. 'These are lovely,' he said, admiring a seascape.

'It used to be a hobby of mine, but I don't get much time for it any more.'

'You painted them?' He sounded genuinely impressed.

She nodded. 'There was a time…long ago…when I wanted to be an artist. But my careers advisor informed me that trying to make a living as a painter is not so easy. So it was either starve in a garret somewhere, or get a real job.'

Rick shook his head wryly. 'Many a great talent has been

squashed like that. You should have paid no attention and followed your heart.'

She grinned. 'And maybe I'd be broke now.'

'And maybe you'd be rich beyond your wildest dreams.'

She met the gleam of amusement in his dark eyes and laughed. 'Thank you for the compliment, but I don't think so. So what about you, Rick? Have you got any secret regrets? Would you have liked to have become a biologist instead of an economist?'

'I can honestly say that is an idea that never crossed my mind,' he said with a grin. 'And I never waste time with regrets. I tend to go out and get what I want in life.'

'And do you always get what you want?' Lucy asked curiously.

'Nearly always.' As their eyes met Lucy felt a strange frisson of awareness. There was a strength about him that said very clearly that this was probably true, and for some reason it unnerved her.

'Lucky you,' she said quietly.

He shrugged. 'I've had my fair share of disappointments.'

Somehow that was harder to believe. Her eyes moved over the solidly handsome physique, the dark, purposeful gleam in his oh, so attractive, sexy eyes. 'What kind of disappointments?'

'Oh, the usual kind…relationships that haven't worked out, that sort of thing.'

'Someone managed to break your heart at school?' she asked impishly.

He laughed at that. 'Well, now you come to mention it, yes, they did actually. Marion Woods.' He shook his head. 'I was seven. She was the love of my life.'

Lucy laughed in turn. 'So what happened?'

'She dumped me for a guy a year older whose parents owned a sweet shop.' He shook his head wryly. 'Just think, if my parents had only owned that sweet shop instead of

their restaurant, we probably would have been married...'
There was a gleam of teasing amusement in his eyes. 'Now
I think about it, it's probably the reason I've grown into the
commitment-phobic, confirmed bachelor you see before you
today.'

'So much for having no regrets,' Lucy laughed. 'That's
a really sad story.'

'Tragic.'

'And are you? A confirmed bachelor, I mean?' Before
she could stop herself Lucy was asking the question.

Rick inclined his head and for a moment his dark eyes
were serious. 'Well, I'm thirty-eight and I've never been
married, so I must be. What about you, Lucy? Has anyone
ever broken your heart?' He looked over at her steadily and
suddenly the mood between them seemed to change away
from the light-hearted.

She wondered how they had managed to skate so abruptly
onto such disturbingly personal ground.

Rick watched the conflicting emotions in her eyes and
knew then that the answer to that was a definite yes. But
then she looked away from him for a moment and when she
glanced back the shadows were successfully hidden. 'Well,
I suppose there was Steve Donnelly when I was in year
three.'

'Childhood has a lot to answer for,' Rick said steadily.

'Can leave you scarred for life,' she agreed.

'So, are you a confirmed bachelor as well?' he asked
lightly.

'I am now. But I had to get married first, just so I could
discover how much that institution didn't suit me.'

'You're divorced?'

Lucy nodded. 'Married for three years, divorced for one.'
She wondered why she had told him that. The strange thing
was he was disturbingly easy to talk to.

'Anyway.' She moved away from the fire. 'You'd better stand here and try and dry off. I'll make us a coffee.'

He smiled at her and as their eyes met her heart seemed to miss a beat.

Hastily she wrenched her eyes away from him and hurried into the small kitchen.

He is a work colleague, she told herself firmly as she flicked on the kettle. And she really didn't need any more complications at work.

Then she caught a glimpse of her reflection in the mirror beside the door and cringed. Her hair was sticking to her head and her face looked unbelievably pale. 'I'm just going to dry my hair, I won't be a minute,' she called, going through to her bedroom.

She was only gone a few minutes, but when she came back she found Rick in the kitchen making the coffee. It seemed strange to see him in there. He had taken off his jacket and the white shirt seemed to emphasise the breadth of his shoulders, the darkness of his hair. Lucy wondered suddenly what it would be like to have a Latin lover. The thought caught her by surprise…shocked her.

He turned to find her watching him from the doorway and grinned. 'I thought I'd make myself at home. Hope you don't mind?'

'No.' She shook her head, but it crossed her mind that the last man who had been in her kitchen making her a drink had been Kris, and that had been just before he'd told her he was leaving her.

'Do you take milk and sugar?' He turned and looked at her again and then frowned. 'Are you okay?'

'Yes, fine.' She smiled brightly, annoyed with herself for letting any memories of Kris into her mind. That man had hurt her more than she had ever been hurt in her life, and she just wanted to forget all about him.

Rick left the cups on the sideboard and walked towards her. 'You looked sad for a moment.'

'Did I?' She shook her head, wishing he would just drop the subject. 'Well, I don't feel sad.'

'Sure?' He reached out and tipped her chin up so that she was forced to meet his eyes.

The impact of his hand against her skin sent wild floods of pure adrenalin pumping through her veins. 'Absolutely sure,' she breathed. And it was true. At this moment she felt anything but upset. What she felt was a wild surge of excitement and desire as her eyes moved over the handsome contours of his face. She wanted him to kiss her, wanted it so badly that she leaned closer. 'Rick.' She whispered his name.

'That's me.' He stroked the silky strands of her mahogany hair back from her face and the next moment his lips were on hers. Lucy had never known anything like the explosion of passion that followed, had never experienced a kiss like it in her life. His lips possessed hers totally and they set such a fire raging inside her that all she could do was lean closer, wind her arms around his neck and surrender to it.

She felt his hands on her waist and his touch seemed to burn through the thin material of her top, making her long for them to move beneath and touch her more intimately. Pressing herself closer, she opened her mouth to the masterful persuasion of his. The sensuality of his tongue against the softness of her lips made her heart beat wildly against her chest, and her senses clamour with dizzy need.

'That was some kiss!' He was the one to pull back; his tone was velvet-smooth with a relaxed, lazy seductiveness.

'Yes.' She stared up at him feeling dazed. 'It was... slightly unreal.'

'Do you think we should try it again?' He murmured the words softly, almost playfully, his eyes on her lips. 'Just to test that it wasn't a figment of our imagination?'

'I think that would be a very good idea,' she agreed and leaned closer to meet his caress. Again as soon as their lips met it was like some explosion inside her. At first the kiss was slow and gently probing. Lucy could feel its effect winding its way insidiously right the way through her body and she felt with each second that passed as if she were falling deeper and deeper into a complete whirlpool of desire until suddenly she couldn't get enough of him…as if he were some kind of drug and she were now totally hooked. Just when she felt she might explode with need, he deepened the kiss.

She was aware that he was the one dictating the pace. He was very much in control and obviously he was a very experienced lover, probably knew all kinds of tricks to turn a woman on. But suddenly nothing else mattered in the world except the desire that had taken complete control of her senses.

Lucy wound her arms around his neck, wanting more, and their kisses entered a new stage, one that was frenzied and wild and totally mind-blowing. She felt his hands on her body, moving more intimately over her now, his hand sliding from her slender waist to the thrust of her breast and every inch of her ached for him to undress her and quench the thirst of her desire.

Then suddenly he stopped and pulled back. She stared up at him breathlessly, her eyes wide with questions—with need.

'Well, I think we've proved one thing beyond doubt…' His voice was husky with emotion. 'We definitely weren't imagining it. The sexual chemistry between us is wild. So much so that I think we'd better stop now because if we carry on I'm going to want to make love to you right here in the kitchen.'

'You're right…' Desperately she tried to pull herself together. But her senses were raging at the interruption and her body was aching with unfulfilled, insistent need.

His gaze flicked over her, taking in the way her body was struggling to get a breath, the way her eyes were clouded with longing and her softly parted lips still swollen with desire. 'There is no doubt about it, believe me. If I kiss you again I'm going to want to take you right here…right now.' For a moment there was naked hunger in his voice.

'And that would be so wrong.' Her voice trembled slightly.

His lips twisted wryly. 'Well, I suppose it depends how you look at it. We are both single…'

'Yes, but it would still be wrong.' She took a deep breath. 'After all, why make love in here when I've got a perfectly comfortable double bed in the next room?'

Even as she said the words she couldn't believe she was saying them. This was the sort of thing her friend Mel might say, but not her.

'Why indeed…?' he drawled, and stroked a hand softly along the side of her face. The touch of his skin against hers made her burn inside with need.

What on earth was wrong with her? she wondered frantically. She had always shied away from transitory affairs and this could be nothing more than that. And she was breaking all her rules about getting involved with a work colleague.

The thought should have brought her back to some semblance of sanity, but strangely it didn't. The trouble was that right at this moment she didn't care about any of that. She wanted him. In fact she couldn't remember ever wanting any man this badly.

So what if he was a work colleague and probably a philanderer…what the heck? she thought as she stood on tiptoe to kiss him again. He would be going back to Barbados in a week.

Just how many complications could one man stir up in a week?

CHAPTER FIVE

LUCY had left the bedside lamp on when she was drying her hair; she wished now that she hadn't. She would rather have had the comforting veil of darkness to hide behind. As soon as she stepped into the bedroom she felt awkward, shy even.

The gold covers on the bed and the gold and damson satin cushions gleamed softly in the subdued light. It was a stylish bedroom filled with period pieces. A Louis XV chair sat in the window and the dressing table held her silver-backed hairbrush and mirror.

Rick pulled her into his arms and there was a look of purpose in his dark eyes that set her heart thundering in her breast. 'Now…where were we?' he murmured.

'I think we were just about here.' She reached up and kissed him softly. For a moment they just stood entwined in each other's arms, then she felt his hand on the buttons of her skirt. 'Shall I turn the light off?' She pulled back from him nervously and made to reach towards the lamp by the side of the bed.

'No, leave it.' He pulled her back and peppered little kisses along her neck. 'I want to see you.' He murmured the words seductively against her ear. 'Want to explore every inch of you.'

Her heart skipped several beats, and the tension inside her spiralled. She wished now she hadn't asked him, had just plunged the room into darkness. He was obviously very experienced and, apart from a boyfriend when she had been at university, she had only ever been with one man—then they had married, and look how that had turned out.

Rick felt her stiffen in his arms. 'Are you okay?'

'Yes...'

He stopped kissing her and tipped her chin up so that he could look deeply into her eyes. There were shadows in their dark green beautiful depths.

'We don't need to go ahead with this if you've changed your mind.' His voice was velvet-soft, so gentle, so infinitely tender that it made her heart turn over with a renewed wave of longing.

'I haven't changed my mind,' she whispered.

He didn't answer her immediately; he still seemed to be studying her very closely.

'Have you got something?' she asked. 'Protection, I mean?'

He smiled. 'Yes...' Tenderly he brushed her hair back from her face. 'Is that what was worrying you?'

She hesitated for just a moment. She didn't want to tell him what had really been going through her mind—didn't want to spoil things by even mentioning Kris's name. That man had ruined enough of her life. So she just nodded.

He kissed the side of her neck. The sensation was overwhelmingly erotic, sending tingles of pleasure all the way through her. Then he kissed the side of her face across her cheekbones before finally capturing her lips. At the same time his hands were moving beneath her jumper, finding the lace of her bra and unhooking it with adept speed.

It was at that point that the last rational thoughts left her mind and sensible thoughts were discarded along with nerves. Suddenly nothing else mattered except the fact that she wanted this man, wanted him urgently—now.

His hands moved possessively over the generous curves of her body and she closed her eyes, giving herself up to the pleasure of his caresses. He pulled her jumper up further and she helped him pull it over her head, her hair falling in glossy wild abandon around her bare shoulders.

Then they were undressing each other. She was unbuttoning his shirt and at the same time she felt his hands unfastening the buttons of her skirt and drawing the zip down. It slithered to the floor leaving her standing before him in just her pants and lace-top stockings.

'You are so beautiful, Lucy,' he murmured, his fingers tracing along the curves of her firm up-tilted breasts. He bent his head and his lips followed the trail of his hands, dusting kisses across her body. The next moment he had swept her up off her feet and was laying her down against the satin cushions of the bed. He kicked off his shoes and joined her on the deep comfort of the double bed.

He had a fabulous physique, she thought as she looked up at him. And suddenly she was very glad that they had left the light on as she drank in the broad power of his shoulders that tapered to a lean waist and lithe hips. She reached up and let her fingers stroke down his chest, touching the hard flat muscles of his stomach. He was in perfect shape. Lucy felt her stomach contract with little darts of excitement and apprehension as he started to unbuckle the belt on his trousers.

'Hurry…' She whispered the word half playfully, and he laughed. Then he reached down and kissed her, with such a seductive kiss that it set her heart racing with pure adrenalin.

His kisses moved across her face and nuzzled in beside her ear as he whispered something to her in Spanish.

'What does that mean?' she murmured, her voice almost incoherent with need.

'It means, patience, my beautiful one. Have patience.' His fingers stroked slowly over her bare breasts, finding the sensitised peaks and toying with them, caressing her until she felt crazy with longing. Then he bent his head and the warmth of his mouth replaced his hands. She felt her body rack with shudders of pure pleasure and she took deep

breaths trying to steady herself. Her hands raked through
the dark thickness of his hair, loving the smooth texture of
it, and then moved down his back, drawing him closer. She
felt as if she could never, ever get close enough to this man.

It was early the next morning when Lucy woke. She was
cradled gently in Rick's arms and she felt warm and comfortable and somehow filled with a wonderful sense of well-
being. It was odd: she didn't really know this man at all, he
was a virtual stranger, and yet lying in his arms she felt safe
and protected and more secure than she had ever done in
her life.

It was just an illusion, she told herself quickly, but for
now it was a very wonderful illusion, and she lay still and
revelled in the warm cocoon, her thoughts drifting hazily
back to the night before and the incredible passion they had
shared.

Rick was a fabulous lover. He had taken her to heights
of pleasure again and again and they were heights she had
never even known existed until last night.

She remembered Mel telling her that it was about time
she took a dive into a little romantic water and that it could
be just what she needed to get her back in the flow. Well,
last night she had felt as if she had taken more than a little
dip—it felt as if some almighty tidal wave had swept her
away. The thought unnerved her slightly. When Kris had
walked out she had sworn that no one would ever get the
opportunity to hurt her like that again and she had meant it.
She still meant it.

She turned restlessly and looked up at Rick, studying his
features. Some people looked vulnerable as they slept, but
Rick still had that air of strength about him. Maybe it was
just the fact that he was so powerfully good-looking. Her
eyes moved from the thick dark length of his lashes to the
sensual curve of his lips, and her stomach tightened suddenly with renewed longing as she remembered how his lips

had felt against the softness of her skin and how wildly he had stirred her senses. Kris had never made her lose control like that…had never swept her away on such a wild ride of exhilaration.

All in your imagination, Lucy, she told herself swiftly. And anyway, maybe she had just blocked out how Kris had made her feel. It wasn't something she wanted to think about.

Last night had been wonderful, but it wasn't anything too special, she told herself firmly. She had to get with the modern programme and start thinking like Mel. It had been just a bit of fun, that was all. And it had probably felt so good because she hadn't done it in such a long time…yes, that could be it. The thought reassured her, made her relax again.

Rick opened his eyes suddenly and she smiled. 'Good morning, lazybones. I was wondering if you were ever going to wake up.'

'Were you now?' His voice was languidly amused. 'Well, you see, the problem was that some young hussy kept me awake well into the small hours.'

'Really?' Lucy grinned and snuggled closer. 'Some people have no scruples.'

'I'm very glad to say that you're right.' He breathed the words huskily and bent to nibble on her ear. It sent a flood of sweet sensations racing through her.

She trailed her hand along the breadth of his shoulders, feeling the strength of his muscles rippling as he rolled her over so that she lay trapped beneath him.

'Last night was fabulous.' He said the words softly as he looked into the beauty of her eyes.

'Yes, it was.' She smiled.

He bent his head and kissed her lips, slowly, possessively. Lucy kissed him back, loving the sensation. And then suddenly they were making love again, only this was nothing like last night. There was none of the wild urgency that had driven them almost senseless...this was different. This was slow and leisurely and tender and somehow much more deeply intimate. Rick looked into her eyes as he entered her, watching her, and then devouring her, tasting the shuddering ecstasy of her lips, taking charge of all of her senses. This was being taken completely...in every sense of the word.

Afterwards she lay in his arms, deeply sated, a feeling of wonderment flooding through her. So much for last night being sensational because she hadn't done it in a long time. She could get used to having Rick in her bed—in her life.

With the thought came the first real sensation of deep unease.

Swiftly she forced herself to pull away from him.

'Where are you going?' he asked, rolling onto his side and watching her as she got out of bed.

'I thought I'd make us a cup of tea.' She picked her silk dressing gown up from a chair and, extremely conscious of his eyes on her naked body, she hurriedly put it on, belting it tightly around her slender waist.

'Actually I prefer coffee in the morning.'

'Do you?' She glanced over at him and it occurred to her again that she knew nothing about this man with whom she had just shared such intimate hours.

'Black, no sugar,' he told her.

'Okay.' It was something of a relief to get out of the room. She couldn't think straight around him. He was too handsome, too disturbingly sensual.

The coffee-cups still sat on the sideboard where he had left them last night. For a moment a vivid replay of how she had invited him into her bed flicked through her mind, making her go hot all over.

It was just sex, she told herself forcefully, no big deal. Okay, she had broken her rules about not getting involved with someone at work, but he would be gone at the end of the week. And as for those weird thoughts about how she could get used to having Rick in her life…well, they were just crazy, passion-induced illusions. Rick was a stranger to her and that was the way she wanted it to stay.

She felt a bit better after the pep talk, stronger, more in control.

She opened cupboard doors searching for some ground coffee, couldn't find any and just settled for instant.

Then the door opened behind her and Rick stood there. He was naked except for a white towel strung low around his waist and obviously he had just had a quick shower because his hair was wet and his broad chest still gleamed with droplets of water. 'How's the coffee coming?'

'Er…fine, all done.' Her heart seemed to be booming in her ears. This was all slightly unreal. Who was this gorgeous man draped just in a towel standing in her kitchen, making himself so much at home?

He strolled over and she hurriedly picked up his cup and handed it to him. 'Thanks.' He took a sip. 'That's good.' He grinned at her. 'Just what I needed after an exhausting night.'

She felt her skin heat up with embarrassing warmth and he laughed. 'I'm just teasing you, Lucy.'

'I know.'

He put his coffee down and caught hold of her before she could move away again. 'We can exhaust each other some more…if you'd like.'

She felt the heat of his arousal through the flimsy material between them and, despite the fact that she tried to hold herself back from him, she felt herself weaken instantly.

She swallowed on a knot in her throat, panic-stricken suddenly by the fact that she wanted this man all over again.

He bent and kissed her, teasingly, tantalizingly, and she responded.

Then suddenly they were kissing passionately and Lucy's

pulses were racing madly and all sensible thoughts had flown out the window.

She felt him untying the belt of her dressing gown, felt his hands moving over her body, and then the next moment he was lifting her up and carrying her back to the bedroom.

It was much later before Lucy could muster up enough energy to think straight. She lay curled up in his arms, wondering breathlessly how their lovemaking could keep getting better.

Her mobile phone buzzed and sleepily she reached out and lifted it. 'I've got a text message,' she murmured, flicking up the screen and peering at it. 'It's from the agency.'

'What agency?' Rick rolled over onto his side and propped himself up on his elbow so that he could look down at her.

'The speed-dating agency.' Lucy pulled up the sheet to cover her breast. It was crazy, Rick had sampled and seen every last inch of her, yet she still felt shy around him. 'Apparently I've got one match.'

'Yes, I know. You're in bed with him.' Rick grinned.

'No…actually this match is with someone called Mark Kirkland,' Lucy said as she scrolled down the message. 'They've sent me his mobile number.' She glanced teasingly up at Rick. 'He must have ticked my box…something you forgot to do.'

'On the contrary, I think I ticked your box several times,' Rick murmured, trailing a hand playfully over the top of the sheet. 'So you'll have to tell Mark that he's just too late. In fact…' he reached and took the phone out of her hand '…you're too busy to tell him anything.'

'Hey! Give me my phone.' She laughed and stretched to get it back, but he held it out of her reach.

'No, you're incommunicado for the morning.'

'Am I indeed?' Lucy looked up at him archly. 'How do you know I don't have a million plans for this morning?'

'And have you?'

'Well…' She felt herself blush. 'I was going to catch up on some housework and I've brought some files home that I need to go through—'

'Lucy!' He grinned at her. 'The housework and the files will have to wait. Because I'm going to ravish you sense-less.' Slowly he bent his head and kissed her teasingly on the lips. Then he drew her down in the bed and took full possession of her mouth, kissing her with mind-altering pas-sion.

The phone dropped to the floor as they both forgot about it.

'You know this is just sex…don't you.' Lucy murmured incoherently when he finally released her.

Rick pulled back from her, one dark eyebrow lifted wryly. 'Well, I didn't think we were playing cards, if that's what you mean. What are you talking about, Lucy?'

'I…' She felt her skin flushing wildly. The words had been playing in her head and she hadn't realised she had spoken them out loud. 'Sorry, that came out all wrong…' she murmured breathlessly. 'It's just that it's a long time since I've done this.'

Rick frowned. 'Done what?'

'This…' He watched as she moistened her lips nervously. 'It's a long time since I went to bed with a man.'

'Oh, I see.' For a moment his dark eyes were watchful. Then he stroked her hair back from her face and the whis-per-soft caress made all her senses tingle. 'How long?'

'I don't know.' Lucy looked away from him, suddenly wishing she hadn't started this conversation.

'Yes, you do. You know exactly.' His voice was quiet.

She tried to pull away from him, but he wouldn't let her go.

'Anyway, the point is that I have this rule about not getting involved with anyone at work.' Hurriedly she tried to move the subject along.

'I know, you told me.' He sounded amused now. 'Looks like you've just broken that rule, doesn't it?'

'No! Not really.' She frowned up at him. 'Because you don't really count, do you? As you said yourself, you'll be leaving at the end of the week.'

'Possibly.'

'What do you mean, "possibly"?' She pulled away from him and sat up, holding the sheet very tightly across her now. 'You told me you were only going to be in the office for a week and then you were going back to Barbados.'

He lay back against the pillows and noted the way her breathing had speeded up, the sudden wariness in her beautiful eyes. 'And I probably am. It just depends how long it takes me to make my final assessments at the office. What are you so afraid of, Lucy?' he asked suddenly.

'I'm not afraid of anything.' She swallowed hard and tried to force herself to sound relaxed. But the truth was that she *was* afraid—afraid of the way he made her feel. She didn't want any man getting under her skin again, and she needed to know in her heart that he was going away soon—that this was just a fling. 'I just…I just don't want what has happened between us to compromise our working relationship. That's all,' she finished carefully.

'You are *so* conscientious,' he murmured with a grin.

She tried to ignore his warmly teasing tone. 'And I don't want us to feel embarrassed around each other on Monday morning.'

'I promise I won't feel embarrassed.' He put one hand on his heart.

She met his eye and had to grin. 'Yes, okay, Rick, you're not the type to get embarrassed by such things. I should have realised that.'

'Yes, you should.' He pulled her down in the bed again, a gleam of purpose in his eyes.

'So, we are clear about our boundaries, then?' She forced herself to say the words even though a molten heat was starting to weaken her resolve.

Rick pulled back for a moment and fixed her with a quizzical gaze. 'What boundaries?'

'Well, for one, that we don't take this into the office.'

'I'm not so sure about that.' He sounded lazily amused for a moment. 'Because, you know, I was kind of looking forward to having sex on the photocopier.'

He watched the way her skin flushed with crimson heat and trailed a cooling hand over her cheekbones. 'Relax, Lucy. I never mix business with pleasure.' For just a second the bantering undertone had gone, replaced with a steely seriousness. 'Work always comes first with me.'

'Well, good.' She nodded. 'It seems we've got something in common, then.'

'So it does.' He trailed a hand over the side of her face. 'You know, you're the first woman I have ever met who is pleased about the fact I put my work first.'

'Good.' She smiled up at him. 'I like to be different.'

'You are different.' He looked into her eyes, liking the spirited way she held his gaze. 'But, you know, the most interesting thing we have in common is this.' He bent and kissed her softly on the lips and instantly a wild passion flared between them.

When he lifted his mouth she was breathless with longing.

'Now, I'm going to make love to you again, and it will have nothing to do with our relationship in the office. The two are entirely separate issues.'

'You're right,' she whispered huskily. 'But don't go reading anything into the fact that I'm letting you stay here in my bed a bit longer,' she added more firmly, and her eyes shimmered with vivid emphasis. 'It doesn't mean anything. Like I said before, this is just sex.'

'Yes, Lucy, it's just sex.' He smiled down at her. 'And it's the first time I've ever had to reassure a woman in this way.'

'I've turned the tables on you, have I? Well, that's good news. I'm all for girl power.' She grinned impishly at him.

'So am I.' He kissed her softly again and she wound her arms around his neck.

A few more hours wouldn't hurt. What were a few hours in the grand scheme of things? And then next week he would be gone.

CHAPTER SIX

LUCY went into the office early on Monday morning. She had slept badly the night before, had tossed and turned wondering how she was going to face Rick at work.

It was all very well trying to act oh, so casual when they were in bed together, telling him that what they had shared was just sex, but in truth she wasn't nearly so blasé. And as soon as he had left her apartment on Saturday afternoon reality had hit her. For one thing she couldn't believe that she had broken all her rules about getting involved with someone at work! What on earth had happened to make her lose her senses like that? She just couldn't understand it.

So here she was at eight-fifteen, calmly trying to arrange her diary. To the outward world she probably looked the personification of calm competence. But inside she felt a complete mess.

Don't be ridiculous, Lucy, she told herself firmly. It was just sex, as Mel would say, no big deal. All she had done was join the modern world.

'Hi, Lucy!' Carolyn put her head around the partition on her way down the corridor. 'How was your weekend?'

'It was fine.' Lucy smiled at her. 'How was yours?'

'Oh, it was lovely. Carl took his first step.'

'Carolyn! It happened when you were home! How wonderful!' Lucy smiled at her friend; pleased for her because she knew she had been worried she might miss that precious first moment with her baby.

'Yes, we were both there.' Carolyn's eyes shimmered with happiness. 'And we got a photo!'

'That's great.'

'And how was the speed dating?' Carolyn asked, suddenly changing the subject.

'It was okay…a bit of fun.'

'Did you meet anybody special?'

'Not really,' Lucy murmured, trying to ignore the strange little flutters of distress. She wasn't lying, she told herself firmly. Rick was very sexy, very nice, but not special to her. The fact that somehow she had spent a whole night and morning in bed with him, and he'd made her feel…well, she didn't want to think about the way he'd made her feel. It wasn't relevant. He wasn't special.

Why couldn't her life be uncomplicated like Carolyn's? she wondered suddenly. She had thought when she'd married Kris that it would be. That they would settle down and live happily ever after with two lovely children and that the weekend would be dedicated to family times… Fiercely she switched her mind away from that. Her marriage hadn't worked. She had tried…heavens, how she had tried…but in the end she had had to just say that she had made a mistake. Married the wrong man. It happened.

'So you didn't meet anyone who made your heart beat even a little bit faster?' Carolyn persisted.

'You are such a romantic, Caro.' Lucy laughed.

'You used to be a romantic too,' Carolyn said softly.

'Maybe.' Lucy shrugged. 'But that seems like a very long time ago.' She was a different person now, she told herself firmly. No one would ever get to her the way Kris had.

But for a moment she remembered how wonderful it felt lying entwined in Rick's arms, giggling, messing about. Abruptly she closed the memory. Rick had kissed her goodbye with a slow, lingering intensity and that, she told herself firmly now, was the end of that. She just hoped it wouldn't interfere with their professional relationship. The big boss was arriving this week and she desperately needed to have her wits about her. She needed this job.

Trying very hard to ignore all the little harbingers of doom, she hit the button on her answer machine to check her messages.

'Hello, Lucy.' A man's deep voice filtered out. 'This is Mark Kirkland. We met Friday night, remember? I hope you don't mind my phoning you on this number, but I haven't been able to get through to you on your mobile and the agency gave me this number as well. I was wondering if you'd like to have dinner with me, either tonight or tomorrow. Give me a ring, will you? My number is…'

'So you did meet somebody!' Carolyn smiled. 'You dark horse, Lucy! I can see I'm going to have to collar Mel for all the juicy details.'

'There are no juicy details!' Lucy said in consternation. But Carolyn wasn't listening. She just smiled as she headed off towards her own desk.

Cringing, Lucy switched off the machine. That message was all she needed to add to her discomfort.

She hoped to high heaven Mel wouldn't say anything about Rick if asked about Friday night. The thought made little butterflies do a clog dance in her stomach.

Trying to forget about that, she rang Mark Kirkland and told him she wouldn't be able to meet him after all and that she was very sorry. It was one less complication in her life, she told herself firmly as she replaced the receiver.

The rest of the staff started to arrive, and Lucy switched her mind to the morning's work.

It wasn't long before computers were on and the usual hustle and bustle of Monday got under way. One of the staff had problems with a crashed program and Lucy went to help her sort it out. She felt immediately better. She could deal with this; she could deal with a thousand problems in the office; and she could deal with seeing Rick Connors…could forget what had happened between them.

Then as she turned around she saw Rick standing watching her, and her calm confidence immediately wavered.

'Morning, Lucy.' He smiled at her.

'Good morning, Mr Connors.' She tried very hard to sound breezily indifferent to him.

He was wearing a dark suit that sat with continental stylishness on his broad shoulders, and he looked incredibly handsome, so much so that Lucy could feel her senses starting to take a dive. Her heart rate increased dramatically as their eyes met and held.

His dark eyes were steady and intense. What was he thinking? Did he find it amusing that she was now calling him Mr Connors? Was he remembering the ease with which he had taken her to bed, the wild passion? Abruptly she tried to switch her mind away from all that as her skin started to heat up.

He smiled, and then his gaze swept over her and she didn't know if it was her imagination, but in a moment he seemed to take in everything about her, from her high heels to the knee-length grey pencil skirt, and pale pink top she wore, to the way she had pinned her long hair back from her face. Then his gaze locked with hers again. 'Did you have a good weekend?'

He was one cool customer, she thought shakily. Far, far too relaxed. She remembered how he had assured her that he wouldn't feel embarrassed today and a sudden thought occurred to her. Maybe he had lied about not mixing business with pleasure. Maybe he was used to it.

She raised her chin a little, determined to be equally sanguine about the situation. 'It was okay.' She forced herself not to flinch away from his scrutiny and noted a flicker of amusement in his eyes.

'Have you been having some problems with the computers?' He stepped nearer.

'Nothing I couldn't fix,' she said quickly.

'Yes, so I noticed. You seem very capable on all levels, Lucy.'

What was that supposed to mean? A few of the staff were flicking interested glances over in Rick's direction now.

'So what can I do for you this morning, Mr Connors?' she said, raising her voice and trying her best to sound very businesslike. She really was going to have to dismiss Friday night from her mind, she told herself very firmly.

'Well, Ms Blake, I'd like it very much if you'd give me a tour of your department and introduce me to your staff,' he said, matching her tone.

She glanced over and saw the flicker of amusement in his dark eyes again. Did he think this was just one big joke? Of course, it was all right for him. He was going back to Barbados soon; she was the one who would be left dealing with the gossip if any of this got out.

Carefully she avoided looking at him and nodded. 'Of course, no problem,' she said lightly, but inside she felt a bit annoyed that her department should be the first to come under scrutiny today.

Linda Fellows' desk was the nearest, so Lucy introduced her first. Lucy was amused to see that she wasn't the only one mesmerised by Rick's good looks. Linda was practically swooning on the spot as Rick spoke to her.

Lucy hoped fervently that her reaction to the man wasn't so obvious.

As each of the women in the room fell like skittles the moment he smiled at them Lucy's manner became more and more efficient. She was very glad that she had caught herself up this morning before she became one more adoring female fan. No man's ego deserved that much stroking, she thought irately.

Rick finished talking to the last of the staff, then turned his attention to the filing systems and the computer programs they were using.

'Perhaps you'd talk me through these.' He glanced over at her as he flicked through different screens.

'Certainly.' She had to go closer to him to use the keyboard. She could smell the tang of his cologne; it brought back intense memories from the weekend…memories of lying in his arms, of feeling his hands moving over her with such sure, sweet sensuality. Her stomach flipped wildly. She tried to move away from him, but it was impossible in front of such a small screen.

As she reached for the mouse her hand collided with his and she felt a shot of electricity flood through her body. Sharply she pulled away.

'Is this the system you usually use?' Rick asked nonchalantly. He seemed totally unaware of the effect he was having on her; in fact he was leaning closer to look at the screen, and for a moment his shoulder rested against hers. She could feel his touch burning through to her very skin.

'Yes. That's about it.' She stepped away from him. 'If you'll excuse me, I've just remembered I have an important phone call to make. Linda will go through the rest of the programs with you.' Lucy smiled over at her colleague and Linda seemed only too pleased to come over to relieve her.

It was a relief to get back to her desk. Lucy wasted some time flicking through her diary, trying to get her heart rate under some kind of control. What on earth was wrong with her? she wondered frantically.

She slanted a surreptitious glance over at Rick as she picked up the phone to make her bogus phone call. He hadn't seemed to mind her leaving him with Linda. She was fluttering around him now, explaining the filing system they used.

Rick smiled at the other woman, thanking her, charm just oozing from him.

Lucy dialled Mel's number.

'Mel Roberts here.' Her friend's helpful tone was an immediate balm.

'Hi, it's me,' Lucy murmured, turning her swivel chair away from the source of her agitation. 'I made a big, big mistake on Friday night.'

'No, you didn't,' Mel said swiftly. 'He was gorgeous.'

'Yes, and now he's running an assessment on my department,' she hissed. 'And I feel totally out of my depth.'

Mel laughed. 'I bet he was good in bed.'

'Mel! Please! I'm feeling bad enough.'

'Maybe you just need second helpings.'

'That's something I definitely don't need. Listen, if Carolyn asks you about Friday night, don't for heaven's sake tell her anything.'

'Of course not. I know you value your privacy, Lucy. I would never say anything.'

Lucy felt awful now for doubting her friend.

Out of the corner of her eye Lucy saw Rick heading towards her. 'So I want the advert to run from tomorrow until the following Tuesday,' she said, switching her tone to a brisk business one.

'Got company?' Mel guessed.

'Yes, that's right.'

'Everything all right, Lucy?' Rick asked nonchalantly and, much to Lucy's consternation, he perched himself on the side of her desk next to her.

'I won't be a moment, Rick,' she said calmly. 'I've just got to place a few adverts before the time deadline.'

'Fine.'

To her consternation he didn't move away, just sat there watching her.

'So have you got that, Ms Barry?' Lucy improvised wildly. 'We want the advert to run for five consecutive weeknights.'

Mel laughed. 'Shall we meet for a drink after work?'

'I think the budget might just stretch to that.'

'Great. Usual place, six-thirty.' Mel put the phone down.

'Sorry about that.' She summoned her best impersonal kind of smile as she turned her attention back to Rick.

Rick smiled. 'I think we need to have an in-depth talk, Lucy,' he said easily.

'Do we?' Her heart jumped nervously against her chest. 'What about?'

'About your advertising budget for next month and the various itineraries that you are promoting at the moment.'

'Oh, I see.' She hoped she wasn't blushing. She had mistakenly thought he was talking on a personal basis. 'Well, yes, of course.'

'Good.' His dark eyes held with hers. 'We'll talk over lunch; shall we say one-thirty?'

Now Lucy was totally wrong-footed. Was this a business lunch or something else? She remembered he had mentioned something about lunch when they had been on the bus together on Friday. Hard to believe now that this man had ever sat with her on a bus...or nibbled her ear so provocatively. Hastily she switched her mind away from all of that.

'Is this a business lunch?' She forced herself to ask the question.

'Absolutely.' He smiled at her.

The smile was the same warm smile that had done dizzying things to her emotions over the weekend.

'That's okay, then.' She tried to sound firmly in control, but in reality she was anything but.

It was almost a relief when Kris walked in.

'Morning, Kris.' Her smile was warmer than usual as she looked up at him. How bad is that? she thought wryly. Any distraction was welcome...even her ex!

'Hi.' He smiled back and for a moment he seemed distracted as he gazed at her. Then swiftly he turned his attention to Rick. 'I have the files ready that you requested. They are waiting for you in Accounts.'

'Great.' Rick stood up from the desk. Lucy noticed how he seemed to tower over her ex.

'If you'd like a more detailed breakdown of each itinerary including cost analysis, I'd be happy to run through things now,' Kris said briskly.

'Thanks, Kris, but I haven't got time,' Rick said easily. He glanced at his watch. 'I have a meeting scheduled. We'll do it later this afternoon.'

'Fine.' Kris nodded.

'See you later, Lucy.' Rick smiled at her.

For a second Lucy smiled back, and then she caught herself up and returned briskly back to her work. No man had a right to have a smile like that, she thought distractedly. It should come with a health-warning sign.

As Rick turned to leave Kris lingered by her desk.

'Was there something else?' Lucy asked him, wishing he would move away and leave her in peace.

'Well, actually, yes. I was wondering if I could have a word.' Kris paused and then to her consternation perched himself on the edge of her desk where Rick had been sitting just a moment ago.

'I'm a bit busy, Kris,' Lucy murmured uncomfortably. She flashed a wary look up at him. 'What's it about?'

'Well, if you're busy maybe it can wait,' he said.

'Okay, see you later,' she said quickly.

He hesitated and she could feel his eyes moving over her.

What on earth was going on in his mind? Since their divorce they had carefully avoided each other whenever possible, always acting with polite civility when they had to speak. Kris had never tried to cross that line before and she was very glad about it. The situation was difficult enough.

Maybe he wanted to tell her about the baby? The thought made her stiffen. She sat up straighter in her chair.

'You know you're looking very well recently, Lucy,' he said suddenly. 'Radiant, almost.'

'Thanks.' Her tone was dismissive. She desperately needed him to go now.

'I am glad we can still be friends, you know.'

'Are you?'

'Yes, of course I am.' He frowned and for a moment there was a flicker of genuine concern in his blue eyes. 'I've always cared about you, Lucy,' he said, lowering his tone to almost a whisper.

It was on the tip of Lucy's tongue to tell him he had a funny way of showing it, but she reined back the sarcasm. 'I really need to get on with work now, Kris,' she said abruptly instead. 'I'm behind with things this morning as it is.'

He nodded, but still didn't move away. 'Maybe we could have a coffee some time?'

She didn't answer him, just turned to her computer and started to tap in some figures.

'You know, I am sorry I hurt you, Lucy.' He whispered the words softly. 'Really I am.'

'It's all in the past, Kris, and maybe it was all for the best. Let's not rake over it.' She didn't take her eyes away from the screen of her computer.

Kris seemed about to say something else, then he shot a look around the office to see if anyone was looking in their direction. A few people hurriedly glanced back at their screens. 'We can't talk in here. Maybe we could meet at lunchtime?'

'I can't.'

'Why not?'

'I'm meeting Rick Connors to go over my advertising budget with him.'

Kris frowned. 'You seem…different around him.'

'Different?' She looked up at him. 'How do you mean?'

He shrugged. 'I can't explain it, but I sense something between you when he looks at you. A frisson of something.'

'Rubbish!' Lucy's heart was thundering against her breast now.

'It's not rubbish. Don't forget, I know you, Lucy…'

'Look, is this leading anywhere? Because I really am busy.' She continued tapping the figures in, but her fingers were hitting the wrong keys now.

'No. I just…never mind.' Kris leaned closer and whispered loudly, 'Look, Lucy, if you want a word of advice then it's this: tread carefully around Rick Connors; I think he's well up in this new company. They say he's a very powerful, very influential man.'

For a second a picture of Rick undressing her flashed into her mind, followed by even more intimate memories of how wildly and how uninhibitedly she had given herself to him. That advice was just a little too late, she thought uncomfortably.

'I'm having a working lunch with him, Kris. Thank you for the advice, but I don't need it.'

'Just trying to be helpful.' To her relief he stood up. 'Okay, well, I'll see you later.'

What on earth was that all about? Lucy wondered as she watched him walk away. That had to be the most she had spoken to Kris in nearly a year.

I sense something between you when he looks at you. A frisson of something. The words played uncomfortably through her mind.

Rubbish, she told herself firmly. Absolute rubbish. And why was Kris suddenly so concerned?

The phone rang next to her and she snapped it up. 'Lucy Blake, how may I help you?'

'Hi, Lucy, it's Rick.'

She felt a sudden rush of disquiet as she heard his smoothly confident tone.

'Lucy, are you there?'

She could hear traffic noises in the background; obviously he was out somewhere and calling her from his mobile.

'Yes, I'm here.'

'I'm stuck in traffic, which means I'm going to be late for my next meeting. So we'll have to reschedule lunch for later. Shall we say two-fifteen?'

'I can't make that,' Lucy told him bluntly. 'I have a few meetings scheduled myself.' She glanced down at the blank pages of her diary and hastily picked up a pencil to scribble in some bogus names. She didn't want to have lunch with Rick Connors. In fact she wanted to run as far as she could in the opposite direction from him.

'Cancel them.' There was no doubting the fact that she had just been issued with an order. Who the hell did he think he was? Lucy wondered angrily.

'That's not so easy—'

'Yes, it is. Just pick up the phone and do it.' Rick's tone brooked no argument. 'I'll send a car for you, be down in the foyer at ten past two.'

The line went dead.

Lucy put the receiver down with a resounding crash and a few people glanced over at her. The nerve of the guy, she thought furiously. Sending a car for her indeed!

CHAPTER SEVEN

SOMEHOW Lucy managed to put in a few hours' work, but her mind kept wandering. First she was thinking about Rick, and the strange effect he had on her. Then she was thinking about Kris and how weird their conversation had been.

She had first met Kris when she was twenty-two. They been attending a two-day seminar; Lucy had been sent by her office, Kris by his. Lucy had to admit the attraction had been instantaneous. He had looked very handsome and trendy and he had made her laugh. They had agreed to meet up when the course was over.

She remembered that first date very clearly. He had picked her up in his bright yellow convertible sports car and had driven her out into the country and they had enjoyed lunch at a picturesque pub sitting by the banks of the River Thames. It had been spring and everything had seemed vibrant and fresh and filled with possibilities.

Kris had reached out and caught hold of her hand across the table and told her how lovely she looked.

He had always known the right things to say, she thought now. She remembered when she had brought him home and introduced him to her parents he had charmed them too.

They had dated for a few years before getting engaged. Then there had been the big white wedding.

She remembered how when they had danced together at their reception he had told her he felt he was the luckiest man in the world, and she had looked up into his eyes and had been so much in love…

A wave of anger flooded through her. Why was she thinking about this now? She had been a fool, an absolute fool.

And, yes, he had seemed so sincere, but it had been an act. As soon as they had been married he had changed.

At first she had put it down to stress. They had taken out a big mortgage to buy the flat and three months later Kris had lost his job. Lucy had remained positive and motivated. After all, Kris was well qualified; she had known he'd get something else. But after six weeks of job-hunting Kris had sunk into a bit of a depression. Nothing he'd been offered had been as good as his old job. Then an opening had come up here, and Lucy had pounced on it for him, had got the forms and, if she was honest, pulled a few strings to get him in.

Things had been better after that, or so she had thought. She remembered how on the day he got the job she had cooked him a special meal and they had opened a bottle of champagne. They had cuddled up in bed later that night and talked about starting a family.

'I love you, Lucy,' he whispered. 'And we'll definitely start thinking about a family some time soon.'

'What about now?' She kissed him playfully.

'Let's just enjoy ourselves for a little while, Lucy. We're not ready yet. And also I think we should get some capital behind us first.'

He knew she wanted a baby but he kept putting her off. It wasn't the right time; work was at a delicate stage; maybe next year when he was more settled…maybe they should wait until he got promoted.

Kris was quite obsessed with the notion of getting further up the company ladder. He worked long hours and gave everything towards getting that promotion but it didn't happen. At the last moment he was bypassed for someone else. Thinking back, that affected their relationship. He was so angry about it, almost as if he blamed her, yet it was nothing to do with her. After that, the subject of a baby was never mentioned again.

There were some people who said that Kris was jealous of her successful career; wasn't able to handle the fact that she was higher up the ladder than him. They said that was why he left her…maybe they were right. Lucy didn't know, although she thought it was probably more to do with the fact that his new partner was a twenty-three-year-old blonde with legs that seemed to go on for ever.

Lucy didn't have a clue about the affair. Yes, he was late home some nights. But he said he was at the gym and she believed him. She wasn't the clinging, suspicious type; she trusted him. Even when he told her he was going away for a week golfing with some friends, she believed him.

It was such a shock when she found out the truth. She felt so stupid, so naïve, so desperately hurt. Even now, when she thought about it, the rawness could strike straight into her heart like a cancer.

Don't think about it, she told herself fiercely. She had made a mistake with Kris; there was no point beating herself up about it.

The buzzer on her phone went. 'Lucy, there is someone waiting for you in Reception,' a voice told her.

She glanced at her watch and got a shock. She was late for her lunch appointment with Rick. 'I'll be right down.'

Hastily she gathered the files that Rick wanted to discuss and, snatching her coat from the stand, hurried downstairs.

Lucy was a bit taken aback when she saw the chauffeur standing in the foyer waiting for her. When Rick had said he'd send someone to collect her she had assumed it would be a taxi.

Followed by some curious glances from the girls on the reception desk, Lucy left the building and slid into the back seat of the stretched limo.

'Mr Connors says if you'd like a drink, then help yourself.' The chauffeur pointed to the drinks bar facing her.

'Er…no, thanks, this is a working lunch,' Lucy told him politely.

The door closed and then he was driving her through the busy streets.

Lucy busied herself sorting through her files and tried not to think about being alone with Rick for lunch. The restaurant would probably be busy and they would just be talking about work. It would be no big deal, she told herself firmly. But every now and then a glimmer of apprehension stirred and she glanced up, wondering where the driver was taking her. She was just about to lean forward to ask him, when to her surprise he turned and pulled up outside Cleary's hotel.

'Here we are, ma'am.' He got out and opened the door for her. 'Mr Connors will be waiting for you inside.'

'Thank you.' Lucy smiled at him and stepped out of the car.

It was one of those days that looked lovely when viewed from inside. There was a bright blue sky and the sun was dazzling, but the air was bitingly cold. Lucy was glad to step into the luxurious warmth of the hotel foyer. She supposed it made sense that their business lunch was here— after all the company owned the hotel—but, even so, it felt strange revisiting the place so soon and she couldn't help but remember what had happened after her last meeting here with Rick. Swiftly she shut that thought away.

'Lucy. Over here.'

She looked over and saw Rick leaning nonchalantly against the reception desk, talking on his mobile phone. He waved to her and she walked towards him.

'I'd like you to get onto that straight away.' He continued with his conversation, but mouthed to her that he wouldn't be long.

She put her heavy files down on the desk and stood patiently waiting. The foyer was busy; there were people checking in and bellboys bringing luggage over towards the lifts. Probably the restaurant would be packed out, she told herself, and the thought comforted her.

'Yes, all right. But make sure it's sorted by Wednesday at the latest.' Lucy noticed he used the same tone he had used with her earlier. It sounded as if he was used to giving orders.

'Sorry about that.' He put his phone away and his eyes moved to the stack of files beside him on the counter. 'I see you've come prepared.' He grinned.

'I brought this year's figures as well as last, so you can compare the logistics.'

'Good thinking.' He smiled at her and picked them up. 'But maybe we'll need an extra-long lunch hour to get through all this.'

'That won't be possible,' Lucy told him quickly. 'I have a meeting in just over an hour and a half.'

'I told you to cancel all your meetings.' His voice was brisk.

'I thought you just meant the ones over lunch!'

Rick shook his head. 'Never mind. If necessary you can ring and cancel from here.'

Lucy wanted to argue with that. Cancelling meetings at the last minute was hardly professional…but as, in reality, she had no meetings and his manner was so authoritative, she closed her mouth again and said nothing.

Instead of following the signs for the restaurant, Rick headed towards a lift on the far side of the room.

'Where are we going?' Lucy watched with mounting concern as he inserted a security card into a slot.

'The company have a suite on the top floor. It will be more private.'

The lift doors swished open.

'I don't see why we need to closet ourselves away up there. Surely the restaurant would be fine—'

'It's too busy, Lucy. We wouldn't be able to concentrate on work in there.' He stepped in and she had no option other than to follow him. The alternative was to make a fuss, draw attention to the fact that her mind was not fully on work, but preoccupied by more personal matters, and she would never admit to that. It was far too embarrassing.

They travelled upwards in silence, Lucy trying her best to avoid eye contact with him.

Rick noticed the way she held herself so straight. His eyes moved over her, taking in the stunning contrast between her creamy skin and the dark luxurious hair. The long dark eyelashes were lowered, the softness of her lips parted. She was an extremely sensuous woman.

'Tell me, Lucy…'

Her eyes flicked up towards him and he noticed the wariness in their green depths.

'Is there any Irish blood in your veins?'

He saw the surprise in her expression and he wondered what she had thought he was going to ask.

'Not to my knowledge, no.' She shrugged. 'Why do you ask?'

'You have the same colouring as my father. His hair was maybe a little darker, but his skin was like yours, pale as alabaster.'

'You're talking about him in the past tense. Is he dead?'

Rick shook his head. 'No, but he's extremely ill. I don't think he'll last the year out.'

'I'm sorry.' She held his gaze for a moment. Lucy was close to her father and she didn't even want to begin to imagine how awful it would be to lose him.

'It's been a pretty rough time. Made worse, I suppose, by the fact that we hadn't spoken for a year before he was diagnosed.'

'How awful!' Lucy frowned. 'Why weren't you speaking?'

'Long story of boring family politics.' Rick shrugged. 'But to cut it short, he wanted me to be married and to produce a son and heir.'

'A bit of old-fashioned thinking,' Lucy murmured.

'Yes, well, he is a bit old-fashioned. I lived with a woman for a few years and it was assumed we would marry. When we didn't he was bitterly disappointed.'

Lucy wondered what had happened, and why he had split up from the woman. Had he walked out on the relationship when the word 'commitment' was raised? She would have liked to ask, but Rick's expression was grim for a second and the subject seemed too intensely personal somehow, so instead she said lightly, 'Marriage is not something you can foist on a person.'

'Yes, and I think you know deep inside when something will work and when it won't,' Rick said seriously.

'Sometimes.' Lucy shrugged and looked away from him again. When she had married Kris she hadn't had any doubts. She hadn't realised what a huge mistake she had made until the last moments of their marriage. 'But sometimes your instincts can be fooled,' she added quietly.

The lift doors swished open and Lucy was distracted from their conversation by the view that greeted her. The ultramodern lounge they stepped out into was vast and there was a wall of glass looking out over a breathtaking panorama of London.

'Gosh, you can see everything from up here, can't you?' Lucy moved across the highly polished wood floor to look out. She could see the London Eye and the Houses of Parliament in the distance, and the River Thames snaking its way through the heart of the city looked as blue as the sky.

'Yes, it's a good view.' Rick put her files down on the chrome and glass side table. 'Would you like a drink?'

'Just a mineral water, please.' She turned and watched as he went to a bar area and got a bottle from the fridge.

'What does the company use this place for?' she asked curiously as she looked around at the white leather settees, the black rugs, and the very expensive abstract paintings.

'Business trips to the City.' Rick handed her drink over and then picked up the files. 'Come on, I'll show you around.'

She followed him, curious to see what was up here.

From the lounge there was a corridor, and through the first door there was a state-of-the-art office complete with flat-screened computers, printers, fax machines. It was probably big enough to accommodate five staff.

'Does the boss bring his own personal team of workers with him when he travels?' Lucy asked.

'Sometimes.' Rick went in and put her files down on one of the desks.

'And what's down here?' Lucy wandered further along the corridor. Next door there was a huge boardroom with a table that would probably have seated thirty people.

'Have you attended many meetings here?' Lucy asked as he joined her by the door.

'A fair few.'

'He likes his gadgets, doesn't he?' Lucy remarked dryly as she noticed the large motorised screen that would probably slide from the ceiling with the touch of a button.

'I suppose he does. That's for watching films of new businesses—'

'And after the film you all sit around and discuss how many jobs should go.'

'Not always.'

Lucy looked up at him in disbelief.

Rick met her eyes steadily. 'Why do I get the feeling you don't approve of your new boss very much?' he drawled.

'Maybe I don't.' Lucy shrugged. 'Let's face it, Rick,

nearly every business that has been taken over by EC Cruises has been divided up. I suppose the word asset-stripper comes to mind.'

'He's a businessman,' Rick said nonchalantly.

'Yes, a cold-blooded, ruthless one.' The words were out before she could stop them.

'I didn't realise you felt so strongly.' His voice was quiet, almost deathly quiet.

'Yes, well, maybe I don't…maybe I'm just concerned about the way things are going to go at the office.' She quickly tried to backtrack. It probably wasn't a good idea to start criticising her new boss; after all, she didn't know how close Rick was to him. What was it Kris had said? *Tread carefully around Rick Connors…he's a very powerful, very influential man.*

Rick smiled. 'Don't try and wriggle away from the truth, Lucy. You don't like EC Cruises.'

'I didn't say that.' Lucy looked up and met the wry expression in Rick's eyes. 'I just…well, I suppose I think they are more interested in profit than people.'

'If a company is to survive it has to be interested in profit; otherwise nobody would have a job.'

'Yes, but it doesn't have to be ruthless,' she said firmly. 'It doesn't have to go out to totally annihilate.'

'And that's what you think we do?'

The quietly asked question made her shift uncomfortably. 'I don't think that of you personally. You're just doing your job.'

'Thanks for the endorsement.' Rick's lips twisted wryly.

She shrugged. 'It's just that I've read a few business reports—'

'You can't always believe what you read.' Rick cut across her swiftly. 'And I suggest you give your new boss a chance to take over properly before you start criticising him.'

'I suppose you're right,' she agreed warily.

'No supposing about it, I am right.' Rick reached out a hand and caught hold of her chin, forcing her to look up and meet his eyes. 'You should definitely give him a chance.'

Although his voice was firm almost to the point of authoritative, the hand on her skin was gentle and it sent immediate shock waves racing through her.

Their eyes held for a moment and she could feel her heart beating painfully against her chest. Then suddenly, instead of thinking about her new boss, she was remembering all the things she shouldn't...like how good it had felt in Rick's arms. Hastily she stepped back from him. 'Well, maybe I'm wrong and I'll give him a chance,' she murmured lightly. 'You know him, after all, and I don't.'

'You could say that.'

'And you like him.'

Rick's lips twisted wryly. 'Let's say he's a man who knows what he wants, and is not afraid to go after it.'

'And do you think there will be redundancies?' She forced herself to concentrate on work and not think about the way he was looking at her.

'I think he will try to avoid them at all costs. But there can be no guarantees, Lucy. Just as there can be no guarantees anywhere in life.'

Lucy nodded, but couldn't help herself from adding dryly, 'I still don't think I like the sound of him.'

'Well, I suppose, we all can't afford your high principles.' Rick held her gaze unwaveringly. 'And maybe there is something you should know—'

The shrill ring of a telephone suddenly cut through the tense atmosphere between them.

Rick hesitated, and then he moved away from her. 'Excuse me. I won't be a moment.'

She watched as he walked away and disappeared back into the office. What had he been about to say? She wandered further along the corridor away from the boardroom and tried not to think about the strange kind of tension that had been spiralling between them. There had been part of her that hadn't wanted to talk about the business or about the new boss, but had just wanted him to take her into his arms again. It was probably what had driven her to be deliberately inflammatory about the new company…it had been a cloak to hide behind. Had she gone too far? she wondered now. Rick hadn't looked amused.

She pushed open a door and found herself looking into a most magnificent bedroom. Obviously no expense had been spared in its décor. The bed was enormous; the floors were polished mahogany. The windows covered the wall and had the same panoramic vista of London as the lounge.

Lucy wandered further inside and looked around the corner at the white marble bathroom with gold taps. She put her glass of water down on the bedside table, and then sat for a moment on the bed. It was a waterbed and it moved seductively under her weight. What kind of a man was her boss? she wondered.

'Lucy.'

Rick's voice from the doorway made her jump. She looked over at him, feeling guilty at being caught snooping.

'Sorry.' She stood up quickly. 'I was being nosy. We should get back to work.'

'I suppose we should.' He moved further into the room and something about the way he was looking at her made her heart miss several beats.

'This is some bedroom.' She tried to sound nonchalant. 'I've never slept on a waterbed.'

'Haven't you?' He moved closer. 'Would you like to sleep on one?' The husky question made her body temperature soar.

She looked over at him uncertainly. 'I hope you're not

suggesting anything improper!' Her shocked tones seemed to echo around the huge room.

He smiled. 'Would I do something like that?'

The teasing gleam in his eye did nothing to allay the wild turmoil flooding through her. 'Probably.'

'You know, you can be very serious, Lucy. And, anyway, weren't you the one who told me it was just sex, no big deal?' He watched the way her cheeks flooded with colour.

'Look, I think maybe you got the wrong idea about me on Friday night,' she said briskly.

'Did I?'

'Yes.' She tried to meet his eyes firmly. 'I don't go in for casual sex. It was a moment of madness.'

'Several moments of madness,' he murmured with a grin.

She glared at him, her eyes sparkling with fire. 'If you were any kind of a gentleman you wouldn't mention that.'

'Wouldn't I?' Rick shook his head. 'Then maybe I'm not any kind of a gentleman.'

'No, you're not.' She put her hand on her hip. 'Look, if it's all the same to you, I just want to forget about what happened between us at the weekend. I wasn't thinking straight. I was upset.' She added the words desperately.

'Were you?' His eyes were serious now the smile had gone. 'Why were you upset?' he asked gently.

'I just was.' She said the words firmly, and hoped that would be the end of the discussion, but Rick still stood between her and the door, watching her, waiting.

'I'd heard some news about my ex-husband, okay?' she said at length, hoping that would suffice.

'And that upset you?'

She nodded. But the awful thing, the really appalling thing, was that deep down she knew she was lying. Okay, she had been upset when she had heard Kris's partner was pregnant, but it had had nothing to do with the way she had fallen into Rick's arms on Friday night. Absolutely nothing.

She had slept with Rick because she had wanted to, because she found him wildly exciting. And probably if he were to touch her now, kiss her…she would fall into his arms and it would happen all over again. The realisation made her heart thump painfully against her chest.

'So what was the news?' Rick asked calmly.

'That's really none of your business.'

'I thought it became my business when you used me for solace.'

'I didn't use you!' She looked over at him, horrified by the suggestion, and he grinned.

'Hey, I'm not complaining. I enjoyed myself.'

Her cheeks glowed bright pink at those words. 'Can we just forget about it now and get back to work?'

'Sure,' he agreed easily.

'Thanks.' Lucy gave him a shadowy smile. She supposed it was no big deal for him; he was probably used to transitory affairs. He obviously just found her attitude towards it highly amusing. That much was clear from the way he was able to joke about it.

'I asked the restaurant to set a table for us in the lounge.' Rick glanced at his watch. 'It should be waiting for us now. Let's go through.'

'Well, I am on a bit of a tight schedule, Rick…' She didn't feel in the least bit hungry. In fact she felt food would probably just stick in her throat. She wanted to keep busy around Rick Connors…needed to keep busy. 'Shall I run through a few items as we eat?'

'By all means.'

He stood back and allowed her to precede him through the door and for just a second his hand rested against her shoulder. She was acutely aware of that fleeting touch; acutely aware that, for all her firm words of protestation, just forgetting about Friday was proving much harder than she had hoped.

CHAPTER EIGHT

It was Thursday afternoon. Only one more day of work and then Rick Connors would be gone. The thought flicked through Lucy's mind as she finished up some letters. She wondered if they would ever see each other again. If they did, it probably wouldn't be for a very long time. Rick's time was probably strictly metered out. She knew EC Cruises had offices in Miami and New York as well as London and Barbados. Well, good, she told herself firmly. All week she'd been trying to avoid him, with little success. Every time she looked up he seemed to be in her line of vision. Talking to someone, laughing with someone… breathing down her department's neck, asking for files, suggesting changes. She'd be glad when he was gone.

Lucy corrected a mistake in the letter and printed it, then sat staring at the blank screen. Would she really be happy when he'd gone? The question sneaked in on her unexpectedly. For a moment she remembered the heat of his kisses, the way he had held her. Then she remembered their lunch together in the hotel suite. Surprisingly it had been quite a relaxed affair. Rick had been businesslike and courteous. They had combed through the files she had brought, and he had asked questions, listening carefully to her replies. They had talked about the general running of the office, Rick asking for her views on things. There had been no reference to their earlier, more embarrassing conversation.

As far as Rick was concerned it was probably all forgotten. And a good job too, she thought fiercely. The new boss was arriving today, and a meeting had been called for four o'clock. The atmosphere throughout the office was tense. There was enough to worry about.

'He's arrived.' Carolyn put her head around the office door to make the dramatic announcement.

There was an instant buzz of conversation. 'What's he like?' Linda Fellows asked curiously.

'About fifty, grey-haired…distinguished.'

'Well, I suppose he would be distinguished. He's a millionaire, isn't he?' Linda murmured. 'I thought he was older than fifty. Someone told me that he was in his late sixties.'

'Yes, I heard that as well…' someone else piped up.

'So where is he now?' Linda asked.

'Closeted in the boardroom with the MD, Rick Connors and a few of the accountants,' Carolyn replied. 'Mr Connors is probably bringing him up to speed with the place, passing on the individual reports he's made on members of staff.'

'I didn't know he was doing individual reports. I thought he was just assessing departments.' Lucy looked up now.

'That's not what I've heard.' Carolyn pulled a face. 'Some staff are going to lose their jobs. Let's face it, it's inevitable in cases like this.'

For a moment Lucy remembered the questions Rick had asked her over lunch about some members of the staff. She had thought it was just a light-hearted, informal chat, but had he been pumping her for information to put in his reports? She frowned and was glad now that she'd been circumspect in her replies.

'Let's not speculate until we've heard what our new boss has to say,' Lucy cut in hurriedly as there was another rumble of panic around the office. But deep down she was a bit worried herself. If Rick was drawing up individual reports, what would he put in hers? Would he mention the negative things she had said about their new boss? As soon as that thought crossed her mind she dismissed it. Rick wouldn't be that petty. And, anyway, all the new company would be concerned about was whether she was doing her job well. And she was, so there was no cause for concern.

Carolyn disappeared back to her own desk. Lucy finished the letter she was working on and passed it over onto her secretary's desk. As usual Gina wasn't there. Probably flirting or gossiping down by the water fountain, Lucy thought wryly.

She came in a few minutes later. 'Have you heard the new boss is here?' she said as she flung herself down in her chair. 'He's in the boardroom.'

'Yes, we've all heard,' Lucy murmured.

'Oh, and Kris says can you spare him a few moments? He's down by the coffee machine.'

Lucy frowned. 'What does he want?'

'Don't know; he didn't say.'

Lucy glanced down at her watch. The staff meeting was in fifteen minutes. 'All right,' she said, getting to her feet.

She didn't know what had got into Kris lately. He had taken to popping into the office to ask her if she was okay. In fact, he seemed to be under her feet every time she moved.

Kris smiled as he saw her heading down the corridor. 'Thanks for coming.'

'That's okay. What do you want, Kris?'

'There's something I think you should know before we go into the staff meeting.'

'And what's that?' Lucy glanced at her watch. 'We'd better be quick. People will be starting to go through in a minute.'

'All isn't as it seems, Lucy.'

'Isn't it?' Lucy frowned.

'No.' Kris took a few steps closer to her and lowered his voice. 'We've all been...I suppose you could say hoodwinked, this week.'

The cryptic tone started to annoy Lucy, or maybe it was

the over-friendly way he was resting his arm around her shoulder as he spoke.

'Just spit it out, Kris. I don't know what you're talking about.' She tried to move away from him, but he held her tightly against him.

'You've spent a fair bit of time with Rick Connors this week, haven't you?'

'No more than anyone else,' she said hastily, and hoped her skin wasn't going red.

Kris looked at her with a raised eyebrow. 'Anyway, I've just come from the boardroom. I had to deliver some papers for the new financial director. And something was said that gave me a hell of a shock. I thought maybe I should run it by you.'

'What was said?' Lucy was really getting tired of this now.

'It was about the new boss. The thing is, he's—'

The boardroom door opened further down the hall and some men stepped out into the corridor. One of them was Rick Connors; Lucy didn't recognise the others.

Rick glanced down towards them, noticing how close Kris was standing to her.

'Kris, did you get the rest of those figures I asked you for?' he asked impatiently.

'Er, not yet.' Kris moved back from Lucy hastily. 'I was just on my way when I got…sidetracked.'

'There isn't time to be sidetracked.' Rick glanced at his gold wrist-watch. 'I suggest you go and get them. And, Lucy, perhaps you'd be good enough to rally your department and get everyone through into the main office ready for our meeting.'

'Yes, of course,' Lucy said smoothly and met his gaze steadily. She wasn't about to be intimidated by him, no matter how cool his gaze, or abrupt his manner.

Kris shot back down the corridor towards his office, but Lucy didn't hurry away.

Rick smiled then, as if her defiant manner amused him somewhat. The gleam of amusement in his eyes irritated her…and so did the fact that her heart seemed to miss a beat as he walked closer.

She glanced at the two men with him, wondering who they were. They were both in their late twenties with dark hair. So neither of them was the boss. One of them smiled at her and his eyes flicked over her slender figure admiringly. She smiled back and was about to return to her desk when Rick halted her.

'Actually, Lucy, could I have a quick word?'

She turned slowly and watched as the two men walked on, leaving them alone.

'After the staff meeting I'd like you to come up to the MD's office.'

'Oh!' Lucy tried very hard not to sound rattled. 'Why is that?'

'Because I want to talk to you about things privately.' Rick glanced at his watch. 'Actually I've been wanting to have a private word with you for the last couple of days but things have just been too hectic.'

'Is this anything to do with the individual reports you've been drawing up?'

Rick looked up at her and smiled. 'Why do you think that?'

'I was just wondering.' She shrugged and then met his eyes directly. 'Have you been drawing up a report on me?'

Rick grinned. 'Actually your report has turned into more of a…tome. I started off with three paragraphs and I'm onto my second notepad now.'

'Very funny, Rick.' Her eyes glinted dangerously green for a second. 'What have you written about me?'

One dark eyebrow lifted sardonically. 'Lucy, I couldn't possibly tell you that.' He smiled. 'It's confidential.'

'And so were some of the things I've told you over the last few days,' she said quickly. 'You seem to find this all very amusing, Rick, but I won't be amused if you have written down any of the things I said about the new boss.'

'Ah, I see…' Rick murmured wryly.

'What do you mean, "Ah, I see"?' She glared at him. 'I mean it, Rick. I don't think it would be fair of you to include my personal observations. And that goes for any comments I've made about staff as well.'

'You've never made any derogatory comments about staff,' Rick countered. 'In fact I've noticed you've gone out of your way to be very fair and very generous in your praise of co-workers. It's a pity the same couldn't be said of your attitude towards the new management.'

'I'm entitled to a personal opinion,' Lucy muttered uncomfortably.

'Yes, you are. And don't worry, I haven't written any of that down on paper…just made a mental note of it up here.' He tapped his head.

Lucy didn't know if that made her feel better or worse.

He watched the flickering light of consternation in her eyes. 'Lucy,' he said firmly. 'There's something—'

They were interrupted as the door of the boardroom opened again. 'Ah, there you are, Mr Connors.' One of the secretaries looked around. 'There is a phone call for you.'

'Can you tell whoever it is I'll ring them back?' Rick said abruptly.

'It's New York and they said it was important.'

A flicker of annoyance passed over Rick's face. 'Okay, I'm coming.' He looked back at Lucy. 'We'll finish this discussion later. Make sure you come straight up to the office after the meeting.'

'Yes, okay.' She turned away from him. 'Yes, sir,' she

muttered sarcastically under her breath, 'Certainly, sir. Three bags damn well full, sir.' Honestly there was something very irritating about that man, she thought as she marched back to her desk. He obviously thought it was very funny to hold the sword of Damocles over her head regarding her comments on the boss. But perhaps the most irritating thing of all was the fact that even as he was giving his orders and winding her up she still was very aware of that undercurrent between them. It was hard to put into coherent words. But there was something…some feeling twisting inside her when he looked at her, when he smiled, when he even raised one eyebrow in that vaguely sardonic way of his.

But she wasn't going to think about that, she told herself crossly, because Rick Connors was trouble with a capital T. He was too close to the new boss and…he'd somehow managed to get too close to her. Way, way too close.

It wasn't until Lucy was filing in with everyone else for the staff meeting that she wondered what Kris had been going to say to her earlier. She saw him briefly at the far side of the room, but the place was so packed with people that it would have been an impossible struggle to get across to him. It had probably been about something and nothing anyway, she thought with a sigh. Kris always had liked to be dramatic.

Mel was over on that side of the room as well; she caught sight of Lucy and waved.

There were no seats left so Lucy found herself jammed back against the wall. The place was hot and airless and filled with the babble of different conversations. But as soon as Rick Connors and his entourage walked in, a hush fell over everything.

They made their way towards the top of the room. There were five of them in all. The two dark-haired younger men, a man with grey hair wearing a silver grey suit who had to be the boss, John Layton, and of course Rick Connors.

It was John Layton who kick-started the meeting off by welcoming everyone and thanking them for their support during the takeover of the business. Lucy wondered if he would stay on as MD or if the new company would want him to retire. She hoped he would stay. He was a decent man and he had always cared a lot about the business. Her eyes flicked along the group towards Rick. He was at least a head taller than the rest of the men. Her eyes drifted over him, noticing how his dark suit was perfectly tailored over the powerful breadth of his shoulders. There was no doubt about it: he was an extremely handsome man and she quite liked being able to feast her eyes on him without anyone noticing. In fact she could have gazed at him all day, and it wasn't just because he was handsome, she thought hazily. There was something powerful about him, something that held her captivated and then pulled at her as if she were a fish at the end of a hook. Rick glanced in her direction and for a moment their eyes met across the crowds. And for just a second it was as if they were alone. The MD's voice seemed to blur into the distance, as did the crowds. And Rick's dark sexy eyes seemed to burn into hers. Maybe she would be sorry when he'd gone, she thought fuzzily. Maybe she'd be extremely sorry…because she was attracted to him, and she would have liked to make love with him again.

The thought sizzled through her.

'And so, ladies and gentlemen, without further ado, I would like to introduce you to the new owner of the company…'

Lucy wrenched her gaze away from Rick, appalled by her thoughts. Firmly she tried to concentrate on what was going on. Her attention winged towards the grey-haired man, waiting for him to step forward. But that man made no attempt to move; instead he was looking around at someone else.

Lucy followed his gaze and skipped over the two younger men. Neither of them was moving either. Then she watched in shocked disbelief as Rick Connors stepped forward.

'...Mr Rick Connors.' John Layton smiled at the other man and they shook hands briefly before Rick turned to look at the crowd.

Lucy wasn't the only one to feel shock; she could sense it rippling around the audience in waves.

'I'd just like to say thank you to John for making this transition period run so smoothly,' Rick said with a smile. 'I've enjoyed my first week here and I've enjoyed meeting all of you and seeing exactly how each department runs. I have to say I've been very impressed with my findings.'

Maybe she had missed something, Lucy thought anxiously. Maybe John Layton hadn't been introducing the new boss...she hadn't really been listening, had been too busy having foolish thoughts about Rick. He wasn't the new boss. He couldn't be. He would have told her...

'And I'd like to apologise if any of you are upset about the fact that I didn't tell you who I was. I always find it breaks the ice and makes things much more relaxed if I can get to know a business from behind the scenes, so to speak.'

Lucy felt slightly sick inside as the realisation dawned. She hadn't made a mistake. Rick Connors was her new boss. She'd slept with her new boss last Friday night, and a moment ago had been fantasising about sleeping with him again!

Suddenly she was frantically flicking through all their conversations in her mind. How she'd told him she didn't like him, that he was ruthless and cold-hearted.

She pictured the way he had looked at her a few moments ago in the corridor. *Don't worry, I haven't written any of that down on paper...just made a mental note...* And, more worryingly: *We'll finish this discussion later. Make sure you come straight up to the office after the meeting.*

Was he going to give her the sack? She wouldn't be surprised. For a second she thought about all the bills she had to pay. When she and Kris had divorced she had bought out his share of the flat, and she had stretched herself to do it. She could probably survive there a couple of months without a job…but no longer. It would have to go on the market.

Lucy felt her hands clenching into tight fists at her side. Through the feeling of sickness, anger was spiralling upwards. She was in this mess because once again she had trusted the wrong man. Rick had lied to her about who he was, probably tried to use her to get inside information about staff…and right at this moment she hated the man, hated him even more than she had once hated Kris. Kris was weak. Rick was…well, she had been right about the new boss all along. He was a ruthless, cold-blooded rat.

'I'm hoping that there will be very few redundancies.' Lucy pricked up her ears and tried to tune into Rick's speech. 'And to that end I have decided to run English Caribbean Cruises as a separate business to EC Cruises. The two will not merge but will be separate in every way. The head office, however, will be based in Barbados, which will mean I will need key members of staff to move over there.'

There was a wild buzz of excited conversation around the room.

'That does not mean that the offices here will close,' Rick cut across the babble in a loudly reassuring tone. 'Now, has anyone any questions?'

A few dozen hands shot up.

'How many people will be transferred to Barbados?' a woman at the front asked.

'That's still to be decided.'

'And what happens if someone is asked to transfer but doesn't want to go?' someone else asked.

'Well, we will try and find key members of staff who do

want to go,' Rick said smoothly. 'Help will be given with the relocation costs.'

Several people were trying to ask questions at the same time now and order was starting to break. Rick held up his hand and people started to hush down again.

'I suggest we leave things there for today, ladies and gentlemen. Thank you for your time.'

There was no arguing with that tone of voice. It was the same commanding tone Lucy had heard him use before. He was a man used to being obeyed. She couldn't believe how stupid she had been, how blind not to see what was staring her in the face. EC Cruises…Enrique Connors Cruises! And then there was that air of powerful authority that sat so easily on his shoulders. She felt so foolish, she didn't know whether to cry or rail against the sheer, infuriating injustice of the fact that if there was a wrong man to get involved with, she sure as hell could pick him.

People were starting to head out of the room and the crowd swept Lucy along with them. She felt so numb inside that she barely noticed Mel waiting for her outside the door.

'What do you think of that?' her friend asked excitedly, drawing her to one side.

'I think I've been a damn fool,' Lucy said furiously.

'Had he not even hinted to you who he was?'

Lucy looked at Mel deprecatingly. 'Do you think if I'd had an idea who he was I would have let last Friday night happen?'

Mel shrugged. 'It wouldn't have made any difference to me. Let's face it, Lucy, he's loaded as well as gorgeous.'

Lucy bit down on her lip.

'Are you okay? You look a bit pale.' Mel looked at her anxiously.

'I'm fine. But I've got to go and face the lion in his den now.' Lucy glanced around and saw Kris heading in her direction. 'Oh, no, he's all I need right now,' she murmured to her friend.

'Lucy…Lucy!' Kris caught up with her before she could disappear into the stream of people still filing past. 'Turn-up for the book or what?' He looked at her pale face and shook his head. 'I tried to tell you earlier, but—'

'But the boss got in the way?' Lucy murmured dryly.

'Did you have any idea Rick Connors was the boss?'

'No, Kris, no idea at all.' Why did everyone think she should know? she wondered angrily.

'Well, I put two and two together as soon as I stepped into the boardroom earlier. That grey-haired man is the financial director, and the two younger men are both lawyers who work for the firm.'

'I see.' Having two lawyers on his team spoke volumes, Lucy thought dryly. Rick Connors probably had everything sorted out to the last letter and there would certainly be no comeback if he sacked her.

'Are you okay? You look a bit pale,' Kris asked anxiously, leaning closer.

'I'm fine.' Why did everyone keep asking her that? She glanced up and saw Rick Connors coming out of the room now, followed by his associates. He glanced over at her and indicated that she should follow him upstairs.

Lucy felt her stomach twisting. She felt as if she were being summoned to the headmaster's study.

'Okay, I'll see you two later.' With a brief smile at Kris and Mel, she headed after him, but by the time she reached the lifts he had already gone up.

Lucy waited patiently for the next lift and then stepped in with the crowd. Everyone was talking about Rick Connors. Who would go to Barbados? How many people would lose their jobs?

At each floor a group stepped out and then she was alone travelling up to the MD's office on the top floor. Would

John Layton be there? God, she hoped so. Lucy glanced at her reflection in the lift mirrors. No wonder everyone had kept asking her if she was okay. She looked terrible. Her skin was white, her eyes shadowed. Come to think about it, she felt physically sick.

Probably nerves. She opened her handbag and hastily reapplied some lipstick, then fluffed up her hair. If she was to maintain some semblance of confidence it was important to look her best.

The lift doors swished open and she stepped out. Lucy could count the number of times she had been up here on one hand. Once for an interview when she had first started to work for the company, once when the company was in dire straits and John Layton had called her up to discuss some of her proposals, and once just after Kris had left her, when she had been going to give her notice in and John Layton had talked her out of it.

She remembered how adamant the MD had been. 'I won't hear of you leaving us, Lucy, it's craziness. We need you here. You enjoy working here, don't you? You have lots of friends here who think the world of you.'

'Yes, but my ex-husband is here and it's…difficult,' she said carefully.

'I understand that and I understand the need for a new start. You've had a shock, Lucy, but they do say that after a shock you shouldn't do anything rash. You should wait at least a year before doing anything that changes your life radically because you might not be thinking straight.'

'I think that would only apply to someone who's been widowed, John,' she said softly.

'Please think about this carefully, Lucy. Wait a while, just a year, and then see how you feel.'

Ironic that just over a year later she should be facing the sack. Lucy stopped outside the door and ran a smoothing hand over her black trouser suit. Maybe she was blowing this out of proportion; maybe Rick wasn't going to sack her. But if not, why had he summoned her up here?

She took a deep breath and knocked on the door.

'Come.'

The authoritative tone from within increased the feeling of anger and tension inside her. It made her wish she hadn't knocked, had just barged in.

'Come in!' the voice called again and hastily she stepped into the room.

Rick was alone, seated behind John Layton's massive desk. In front of him were piles of documents and files. He was flicking through them and at the same time talking to someone on his cell phone. His voice seemed to echo slightly in the cavernous room.

'Yes, the lawyers have been over them and I got the okay this morning. No, I've sent copies to the New York office. So I don't know why we've got a problem.' He glanced up at Lucy and indicated that she should take the seat opposite. Then he continued to rummage through the paperwork in front of him. 'No, Cindy is off with personal problems so I'm minus my PA at the moment.'

Lucy made no attempt to sit down on the chair he had indicated, she just continued to stand at the other side of the table watching him. How had she been so stupid? she asked herself angrily. How had she missed that air of power that sat so easily on his shoulders? The expensive suits, the stylish haircut…everything about him screamed success and money.

She remembered the way he had laughingly told her that, although he was staying at Cleary's, his room was little better than a broom cupboard.

And she had believed him!

How he must have laughed about that as he'd showed her around his penthouse suite the other day. In fact she had probably just been one big joke to him all along.

'Lucy, are you going to sit down or are you going to stand there glaring at me all day?' he asked as he put the phone down.

His calm demeanour only served to make her angrier. She fixed him with a steady, blazing gaze. 'That depends. Is it worth my sitting down or are you just going to fire me?' she asked tightly.

'Fire you?' He leaned back in his chair and once more there was that dark glint of amusement in his eyes that really irritated her. 'Why would I fire you?'

The question should have helped calm her nerves, but she was too angry to feel any sense of relief.

'Because I told you I don't like you, or the way you do business.'

Rick shrugged. 'I thought we'd agreed that you were going to give your new boss a chance before you passed judgement.'

'That was before I knew who he was,' Lucy murmured. Her eyes narrowed on him. 'You told me a pack of lies.'

'That's a slight exaggeration, Lucy,' he said easily. 'I just didn't tell you the whole truth.'

'In my book, that's lying.' She rested one hand on the desk and leaned closer. 'If you went to bed with someone and casually didn't mention the fact you'd got a wife and three children, would that not be lying either?'

'No, of course that would be lying.' He frowned. 'But I haven't got a wife or three children.'

She looked away from him, wishing for some reason she hadn't said that. She didn't want him to get the wrong idea and think she cared on any deep emotional level about his lies.

'Well, I don't much care for your behaviour,' she said quickly, her tone calm and icy cool. 'You knew I had reservations about sleeping with you because of the fact that I was working with you this week. So you should have stopped to think how much more uncomfortable I'd feel when I found out I'd slept with my boss.'

'I wasn't your boss at the weekend, Lucy,' he said quietly. 'I think we transcended beyond what job titles we have. We were ourselves and it felt special.'

She stared at him and for a moment her heart beat rapidly and painfully against her chest. She remembered the way he had held her, the way he had kissed her…the way he had made her feel alive and cherished. Then hastily she blanked out the memory. 'It was just a roll in the sack,' she said carefully. 'We both know that. So you can cut the charm, Rick. I didn't want or expect anything from you. But it would have been nice if you'd been honest with me.'

For a fleeting second Rick glimpsed a raw vulnerability in her, then it was gone, replaced by a flush of heat on her high cheekbones, a blaze of fire in her green eyes.

'Anyway…' she looked away from him, cross with herself for mentioning what had happened between them '…I'm sure you haven't summoned me up here to rake over all that, and I certainly want to forget it—'

'Lucy, sit down.' He cut across her gently. 'I'm sorry you feel hurt by the fact that I didn't tell you who I was—'

'Not hurt, cross,' she interrupted him firmly, and he smiled.

'Believe it or not, I did intend to have a word with you before the meeting today, but it's just been hectic.' As if to prove his point, his phone rang again. Impatiently he reached to pick it up.

Lucy listened as he had a brusque conversation with someone who should have received some vital papers and hadn't. She supposed she shouldn't have allowed herself to lose her temper, not if she wanted to keep her job. And as for mentioning the fact that they'd slept together—that was a big mistake. That should all be forgotten. Rick Connors certainly wasn't wasting any energy thinking about it; why should she?

She sat down in the chair beside her.

'Sorry about that.' Rick put the phone down. 'Now, where were we? Oh, yes. I didn't tell you who I was straight away because I wanted complete confidentiality to assess this office, and also…I liked the way you acted so naturally around me, said exactly what you thought.' He watched the way her eyebrows rose and grinned. 'Yes, even when I didn't agree with you.'

'You were picking my brains, using me as a kind of spy. That's why you were asking me my thoughts on the running of the office—'

'Lucy.' He cut across her firmly. 'I was asking your opinion because I want you to go out to Barbados for a year and help set up the new offices.'

Lucy stared at him blankly.

'That's why I asked you to come up here. So we can discuss it.' He glanced at his watch. 'But unfortunately I'm running out of time.'

The phone rang again and he shook his head and picked it up. 'Yes…just forget about it. I'll fly back via the New York office today and sort it out myself.' He slammed the receiver back down again and stared at Lucy. 'So what do you think?' he asked as if they hadn't been interrupted.

'Well…' Lucy shrugged. In the space of just a few minutes she had gone from thinking she was being sacked to being offered what sounded like a promotion. 'I'm not sure.'

'I'll tell you what.' Rick glanced at his watch again. 'I'll get my secretary to organise some tickets for you. You can fly out…' He reached for a calendar and flicked over the pages. 'I'm going to be stuck in New York for at least a week…so say the beginning of next month?' He glanced back at her. 'In fact, that should be good timing. We're organising a three-day cruise launch party for the managers and hierarchy in the company to mark the takeover of this London office. You can join me for it and lend a hand with some of the last-minute organisation details.'

Join him on a three-day cruise! As their eyes locked across the table she felt a shiver run through her that was half apprehension, half exhilaration. Was this strictly business? If it wasn't, maybe she shouldn't go. She was already out of her depth. 'Rick, I—'

'Then you can stay out there a week and look over the new offices, see what you think,' he continued firmly. It didn't sound as if he was asking her…he was telling her.

Before she could say anything the buzzer on his desk rang. 'Honey, I'm down in Reception waiting for you,' a huskily attractive woman's voice cut into the silence.

Rick grinned and reached to press the button to reply. 'I'll be right down, Karina.'

Now, who was that? By the sounds of it, whoever it was was close…very close. And to think she had worried— imagined—that Rick might have been asking her to join him on that cruise for reasons other than business! Really, sometimes she was incredibly naïve. Rick had taken her to bed; he was onto his next conquest now.

'I'll have to go, Lucy.' Rick looked across at her steadily. 'I'm leaving London late tonight.'

'Well, I hope you have a pleasant flight,' Lucy told him coolly.

He smiled as if her coolness amused him. 'I'll see you in Barbados,' he said firmly.

For just a second she hesitated and then she nodded. What had she got to lose? It was a possible promotion, or at worst ten days in the Tropics. 'I'll see you in Barbados.' She slid the chair back and walked from the room without a backward glance.

CHAPTER NINE

THE plane was circling. Beneath her Lucy could see the vivid turquoise of the Caribbean Sea and her senses soared. Despite all her initial misgivings, she was glad she had come. This had to beat sitting in the cold grey surroundings of the miserable English climate, and it was only for ten days. She could handle seeing Rick again for ten days. Her stomach skipped at the thought as the plane banked and started its final descent.

It was three and a half weeks since she had last seen Rick. She knew he had been in New York for two of those weeks, because he had phoned her at the office to check she had got her tickets and to run through a few of the details for the trip.

It had been really strange picking up the phone and hearing his voice again, especially as she had been sitting at her desk thinking about him at the time, wondering where he was, what he was doing. Not that she cared, of course. She was just curious.

Their conversation had been very businesslike. It was only when they had finished discussing work that he had asked her how she was. 'I'm fine,' she answered airily. 'How are you?'

'Cold. It's snowing here. I'm looking forward to getting back to Barbados.'

'It's a tough life,' she said, idly drawing circles on a blank piece of paper. 'And I suppose the company have installed you in another broom closet.' She hadn't been able to resist the mischievous jibe.

He laughed at that. 'Afraid so, and it's worse than the last.'

'That bad?' Lucy grinned. 'I just hope they aren't going to install me anywhere as grim as that in Barbados…which reminds me. I haven't had any hotel vouchers or reservation details.'

'That's because you're not staying in a hotel. I figured you may as well stay on board the *Contessa*. You'll be on there for three nights anyway and it will be docked near the offices so it will be handy.'

'Okay.' Lucy was quite happy with that. She knew the *Contessa* was a first-class ship. Even the staff quarters were luxurious, so ten days on board would be no hardship. 'I'll take a taxi down there when I arrive.'

'No, I'll send someone to collect you,' Rick said firmly. 'You'll need a security pass for the docks.'

The plane bounced down onto the runway.

'Welcome to Barbados,' the air hostess said as people started to gather their belongings. 'The local time is four-fifteen and the outside temperature is thirty degrees.'

Lucy smiled to herself and put the jacket she had worn on the way to Heathrow into her hand luggage. It didn't sound as if she would need it again for ten whole days.

The heat hit her as soon she stepped out of the aircraft; the sky was clear blue and even the breeze that ruffled her hair was warm. She was glad now that she had changed out of her jeans and into a lightweight dress.

It didn't take long to clear Immigration, and because her luggage was going to be transferred directly to the cruise ship she headed straight out into the arrivals hall and scanned the name boards held up by people waiting for passengers. Her name was nowhere in sight and she was just about to head towards an information desk when she turned and saw Rick walking towards her. She felt a jolt of surprise and also something else, something far more disturbing—a twist of excitement and longing that made her insides wrench.

Trying very hard to ignore the feeling, she put a bright smile on her face. 'Hello, this is a surprise. I didn't expect to see you here.'

'Hello, Lucy.' To her consternation he bent and kissed her on the cheek. The familiar scent of his cologne and the touch of his lips against her skin brought back a rush of memories from their night together, and made her heart race unsteadily against her chest.

'Did you have a good journey?' He reached to take her hand luggage from her.

'Yes, it was pleasant. I managed to sleep for a few hours.' She was very conscious now of the way he was looking at her, and she was really glad that she had spent time freshening and tidying her appearance before landing. At least her hair and make-up were passable.

As always he looked incredibly good. She had never seen him dressed so casually; he was wearing a lightweight pair of beige trousers and a short-sleeved shirt in the same colour. He looked tall and bronzed and powerfully handsome. She tried very hard not to notice the effect he had on her.

'Come on, then, I'm just parked outside.' He strode away from her, leading the way out into the brightness of the sunshine.

'Wow, it's hot,' she murmured as they stopped next to his bright red Porsche.

'Is that a complaint?' He stowed her bag away in the boot and grinned over at her.

'After the weather I've left, certainly not.' She got into the car, settling herself in the deep leather seats appreciatively. 'So what brings you all the way out here to collect me?' she asked lightly as he got behind the driving wheel. 'Got no chauffeur today?'

Rick glanced across at her. 'Nowhere is very far away on Barbados. And I was heading down to the ship anyway.'

'Well, it's very good of you, thanks,' she said quickly, not wanting to sound ungrateful.

'But you'd rather I'd sent the chauffeur,' Rick said wryly as he started the engine. 'Do I intimidate you, Lucy?'

'No, of course not.' She looked over at him with a frown.

'I didn't think so,' he said with a smile. 'So why do you jump a mile every time I come close?'

The casually asked question took her by surprise. 'I wasn't aware I did.'

He glanced across at her with a raised brow and she felt herself blush to the roots of her hair. 'Okay, maybe I do.' She shrugged. 'I don't know why. Nobody else makes me do that. Maybe it's just you…you have a weird effect on me.'

His lips twisted wryly for a moment. 'You have a bit of an unsettling effect on me, too. You irritate the hell out of me sometimes, you're so infuriating, and sometimes…' The engine started with a powerful roar, cutting off his words so that she wasn't sure if he'd finished that sentence or not.

'And sometimes?' She looked over at him curiously. 'I didn't hear what you said.'

'Didn't you?' He grinned and then slipped the car into gear. 'Maybe it's just as well. We do have to work together after all.'

Lucy glanced out of the window, tried to concentrate on the passing scenery and not on his words…but she was fighting a losing battle. She was consumed with curiosity. 'So, in what way do you find me infuriating, exactly?' she probed.

'Hard to put a finger on it…exactly.' He glanced over at her and his eyes gleamed with amusement. 'I'll tell you next time it happens.'

'Well, gee, thanks,' she muttered sarcastically. 'I suppose you don't like the fact that I tend to say what I think.'

'No, I told you, on the whole I like that about you. It's very refreshing.' He grinned. 'Except of course for the times when you are being less than complimentary about your boss.'

'Yes, well. I'm sorry about that.' She cringed a little at the reference. Would she ever live down those remarks? she wondered uncomfortably. 'It seems I was wrong about you.'

'Were you?' He glanced over at her.

'Well, you haven't dissected the company and sacked half the workforce, have you? At least, not yet. So I must have been wrong.'

He smiled. 'That's a very wary apology, if I may say so.'

'Is it?' She shrugged. 'Well, don't take it personally. Maybe I'm just a wary person.'

'Yes…' He looked at her, and for a moment his eyes were serious. 'I think perhaps you are. Obviously a person has to work at gaining your trust.'

'Maybe.' She conceded the point. 'And we didn't exactly get off to a good start, did we?'

'Didn't we?'

She wished she hadn't looked over at him just then because as their eyes met she felt herself blush wildly. 'I was referring to the fact that you lied about who you were,' she said stiffly, trying very hard not to remember their time together in bed.

'Ah. I see.' He nodded. 'Well, I'm sorry about that. Maybe we are both similar characters…both quite wary.' He changed down a gear and the car slowed as it approached a town. 'So, in this new light of reconciliation, shall we bury the past and start again?'

She shrugged. 'Yes, of course. I think it's important that we have a good working relationship.'

'Me too.' He smiled at her.

Something about the way he looked at her made something stir inside her, some kind of longing that was wildly preposterous. Hastily she looked away from him. He was her boss. They had turned a corner away from all of that, she told herself firmly.

'So where are we now?' she asked, changing the subject.

'This is Bridgetown, the island's capital.'

With the suddenness of the Tropics it had started to go dark now. Lucy had an impression of quite a small town with old colonial-type buildings. Fairy lights twinkled along their roofs and on trees in the park.

'In case you're wondering, they still have some of their Christmas decorations up,' Rick said with a grin as she noticed a reindeer lit up on a roof. 'They don't have the same sense of urgency about taking them down within twelve days as they do in England. In fact they don't tend to have a sense of urgency about anything, really. It's all very laid-back here.'

'That's nice.' Lucy smiled. 'Wish I could be that laid-back, but I'm very superstitious. If I didn't take down my decorations in time I'd worry that I was storing up bad luck for the rest of the year.'

'Really?' Rick looked over at her. 'I didn't have you pegged as the superstitious type.'

'Oh, yes. I always throw salt over my shoulder if I spill some.'

He laughed. 'But, Lucy, all those things are just based on practicalities. Salt used to be expensive; that's why it was bad luck to spill it.'

'I know all that.' She shook her head. 'But I don't want to tempt fate so I have all sorts of little idiosyncrasies.'

Rick grinned. 'That sounds interesting. You'll have to tell me more over dinner.'

'Dinner?' She looked over at him sharply.

'You know, that meal you eat with a knife and fork, taking care not to spill any salt.' He smiled at her.

'I'm a bit tired, Rick,' she said cautiously.

He nodded. 'I'm sure you are, it's a long flight. But you should eat something. The *Contessa* is fully staffed and stocked up…and tonight we'll be the only passengers on board so we should take advantage of the situation and relax.'

'We'll be the only passengers?' She looked over at him in surprise and felt a momentary tingle of alarm. 'I didn't know you were staying on board the ship? I thought you would be staying at your own house.'

'I thought I might as well stay on board this evening. I've got a lot of last minute work to do down here in the morning and then in the afternoon the managerial staff and VIPs will be arriving for the three-day cruise.'

Rick stopped at a security checkpoint for the piers and flashed a pass at the man on the gate.

'Evening, Mr Connors.' The man smiled and the electric barrier immediately lifted to allow them through.

As they drove down towards the berth Lucy had her first glimpse of the *Contessa* lit up against the night sky. She was a magnificent-looking ship, small by cruising standards; she carried more crew than passengers and was aimed at the luxury end of the market.

Rick parked the car down by the end of the quay and Lucy stepped out into the night air. It was a soft, sultry evening and the breeze that ruffled in over the calm dark water of the Caribbean did nothing to alleviate the stickiness of the temperature.

Lucy couldn't get over how quiet it was. When she had visited ships in Miami the docks had always been bustling with people; here there was just one member of staff waiting for them by the end of the gangplank. They walked up and into the cool, air-conditioned interior and stepped straight into the main foyer, a vast space with a gold staircase that branched off into two and circled the upstairs gallery. There were shops and a reception desk and a row of glass-fronted lifts.

Rick led the way into one of the lifts and pushed the button for the top floor.

'Have you been on board the *Contessa* before?'

She shook her head. 'No, but I did an assessment of her last year for the new brochure, so I feel I know her very well. She's an Italian ship, isn't she?'

Rick nodded. 'Yes, and finished with a lot of style. I think the management will enjoy their party cruise.'

'I'm sure they will. And I believe there is another party to launch the takeover of the company for the rest of the London staff at Cleary's next month?'

Rick grinned over at her. 'Well, you know how I like to keep my staff happy.'

'And of course it's all tax deductible,' Lucy said with a wry smile, in case he thought that she was fooled into thinking he was completely altruistic.

'Ah…rumbled again.' Rick laughed. 'It's very hard trying to shake off my ruthless image with someone like you around, Lucy. Let's hope I have better luck with the journalists I've invited along.'

Lucy met his eyes and smiled. It had been her idea to invite some members of the press; she had thought it would be a good move because hopefully they'd get some favourable write-ups in the travel columns. 'Knowing how charming you can be, I'm sure it will be quite a PR triumph.'

'Do you know, I think that's the nicest thing you've ever said to me,' he said teasingly. The lift doors swished open and Rick led the way down the corridor and then inserted a card into a door and swung it open to reveal a very large and elegant suite.

'This is lovely.' Lucy wandered across the lounge area to

look out of French windows that opened onto a private balcony.

'Your room is through here.' Rick opened a door to her left and she could see a large cabin decorated in shades of rose and cream with a double bed and another door out towards the balcony and one towards the corridor.

'This is very luxurious. I expected to be in staff quarters.'

'Now, what kind of a boss do you think I am?' Rick asked. 'No, I want you here where I can keep an eye on you. We've got lots of work to do.'

'And where will you be staying?' Lucy asked guardedly.

Rick opened the door on the other side of the lounge to reveal an identical cabin to hers, only at one side of the room there was a desk piled up with papers.

'I see.' She felt a flicker of apprehension at working in such close proximity to him, but the thing that worried her most was her own will-power and ability to keep things businesslike. She was sure he would have no problems with it, after all he was a businessman and she knew he had the ability to put work in front of all else. He had probably dismissed anything on a personal level between them long ago, right to the back of his mind. So why couldn't she?

Why was it that as soon as she was in his company common sense seemed to fade into the background? For some reason he only had to look at her to play complete havoc with her emotions.

No other man had ever had this effect on her before and she really hated herself for it. But, being fair, she supposed most women would feel the same. Rick was just too attractive. She was sure those dark eyes alone could melt any woman's resistance in seconds.

There was a knock at the door. 'That will be your luggage,' Rick said as he went to answer it.

A porter brought in her case and placed it in her bedroom. Rick glanced at his watch. 'I've got some business to

attend to up on the bridge, so I'll leave you to settle in and
I'll see you on deck five for dinner. Shall we say in about
an hour?'

She nodded, and he smiled at her in that warm, disarming
way of his. It had an immediate and strong effect on her
pulse rate and as soon as the door closed behind him she
had to sink down into one of the comfortable armchairs.
Given the way Rick made her feel, it was probably a very
bad idea having dinner alone with him. But what else could
she do? It wasn't like a date that you could turn down; it
was dinner with the boss. She had to go.

Lucy leaned her head back and closed her eyes. Who was
she kidding? she asked herself crossly. She wanted to have
dinner with him. Every little fibre of her soul seemed to
zing with a curious feeling of excitement just at the thought
of being in his company.

Her eyes flew open. Every time he smiled at her, she
wanted him; every time his hand so much as brushed against
hers it sent tremors of awareness racing through her. A sudden feeling of sickness twisted inside her. It was nerves, she
supposed; nerves because she knew how foolish she was
being. Rick was off limits; he was her boss...and anyway
he wasn't interested in her. He had moved on to other pas-
tures.

Lucy stood up and went through to her cabin to unpack.
She was furious with herself for allowing such weak feelings of desire to flood through her. Rick had lied to her
about who he was, for heaven's sake. How could she have
any feelings for a man like that? She couldn't trust him...

She unpacked haphazardly, throwing things into drawers
and cupboards, then went into the *en suite* bathroom to
shower.

'And he's probably an incorrigible womaniser,' she told
herself as she lifted her head to the powerful jet of water.
Probably had more women than she'd had cups of tea. With

his looks and money they were in all probability throwing themselves at him all the time. She remembered the huskily sexy voice of the woman who had spoken to him at the office. What was her name…Karina? Not for the first time, she wondered who she was. Not that she cared, of course, because one thing was for sure, she wasn't going to be another one of his harem. She had far too much pride and common sense for that.

A little while later, wearing a buttercup-yellow summer dress and a matching pair of high heels, Lucy made her way up to the fifth deck to have dinner with Rick. She stepped out of the lift, her head held high, a defiant gleam in her green eyes. She wasn't going to be swayed towards dark feelings of desire for Rick ever again. That was an end to it. She was going to be sensible and from now on become immune to him.

There was a member of staff standing outside the lift. 'Good evening, Ms Blake. Mr Connors is waiting for you in the restaurant, if you'd like to follow me.'

'Thank you.' She followed the man towards some doors, which he held open for her, and then she stepped out onto the deck and found herself in the open-air restaurant at the back of the ship. The heat of the tropical night was soft against her skin and pleasant after the cool of the air-conditioning.

Candlelight flickered on the fresh white tablecloths and music played gently in the background. Rick was sitting at a table by some open rails and behind him the lights of Barbados twinkled invitingly. He stood up as he saw her walking towards him and she noticed he had changed into a dark suit with a white shirt. He looked very handsome— in fact, so handsome that she could feel all her firm intentions wavering dangerously.

He smiled at her as she reached his side and she could

almost feel his eyes as they swept appraisingly over her. 'You look lovely, Lucy.'

'Thank you.' She sat down in the chair that one of the waiters pulled out for her. 'This is very unexpected. I thought we would be having a quick snack in the pizzeria on the other side.'

'I thought this would be a little more relaxing.' Rick took his seat opposite her again. 'After a long, tiring flight it's good to sit back and be pampered.' He passed a menu across to her. 'Now, what can I get you to drink?' he asked solicitously. 'Would you like white wine or would you prefer something else?'

Lucy glanced over at his glass and noticed he was drinking white wine. 'I'll have the same as you.'

She watched as he lifted the bottle from the cool-bucket next to him and poured her a glass.

'So did you see to all your business on the bridge?' she asked briskly, trying very hard to steer the mood of the evening towards sensible and away from seductive, but it felt like an uphill task against the candlelight and the soft music and the gentle swish of the sea against the ship.

'Yes, all done. We are all ready to take our passengers onboard tomorrow.'

'The ship seems eerily quiet.' She sipped her wine and looked around at the deserted restaurant. 'It's a bit like being on the *Marie Celeste*.'

'Do you think so?' His lips twisted in a wry smile. 'If no waiter comes to take our order I'll start to worry. But I thought it was rather pleasant myself, like the calm before the storm. Because at approximately three o'clock tomorrow afternoon, over one hundred members of the management team will be descending on us.'

'Should be fun.'

Rick shrugged. 'I hope so. I'm just glad you're here to

help, especially as my personal assistant is off work at the moment.'

'What exactly do you want me to do?' Lucy asked, taking a sip of her wine.

'Just meet and greet all of the passengers, and generally act as hostess for the trip.'

'Oh?' Lucy looked over at him in surprise. 'I would have thought that was a job for your girlfriend.'

Rick laughed at that. 'Well, I was kind of hoping that you'd act as a bit of a go-between. You know all of the top management from your side of the company very well, Lucy. So you'll be able to prompt me if I forget a name and help me with the introductions between them and the EC Cruises crowd.'

'That's no problem.' She nodded.

'And I could also do with some help sorting through my paperwork, ready for some discussions I will be having later. My desk is in a bit of disorder at the moment.'

Lucy laughed. 'If that's the desk I glimpsed through the open door of your cabin, then I think chaotic would be a better description.'

'I was hoping you hadn't spotted that.' He grinned.

A waiter arrived to take their order and Lucy hastily glanced at the menu. There was a large choice, but after all the travelling she only wanted something light so she selected a simple starter of melon with Parma ham and steak with a green salad.

'So how were things at the office when you left?' Rick asked once they were on their own again.

'Ticking along nicely. Everyone has been in better spirits since learning you're not closing the London office.'

'And what about Kris Bradshaw? Is he in better spirits these days?'

The quietly asked question took her by surprise. 'Kris?'

She shrugged and tried to look impassive. 'I don't know. I suppose so. Why do you ask?'

'I guess I'm just curious. I noticed that he seemed to be around you a lot in the office. And then someone informed me that he was your ex-husband.'

'Who told you that?' Lucy could feel herself growing hot inside. She didn't want to talk about Kris; it was too personal.

'Does it matter who told me?' Rick murmured quietly. 'The thing is, you didn't tell me.'

'I didn't think it was relevant. Yes, he's my ex-husband, but it doesn't interfere with my work in any way, so there's not much else to say.'

Rick seemed to be watching her very intently. 'But will it interfere with your decision on whether or not you take the job here in Barbados?'

'No, of course not!' Lucy was taken aback by the question. 'He's my *ex*-husband, Rick. He left me for another woman and we have nothing to do with each other any more.'

'But you still love him.'

Lucy stared at him, unsure if that quietly worded sentence was a statement or a question. 'No, of course not!' Her heart bounced unsteadily against her chest. 'I'd have to be crazy to still love Kris after the way he walked out. I don't know why you would even think such a thing!'

Rick watched the shadows flicker across her face, the way her eyes darkened to deepest jade. He had definitely hit a raw nerve.

'I'm just repeating the gossip that was flying around the office, Lucy.'

'I didn't have you pegged as the type of person who'd listen to gossip.' She glared at him.

'It was hard to avoid, and I suppose my ears pricked up

when I heard people mentioning the fact that you had gone speed dating.'

'People were talking about that?' Her skin blanched. 'They don't know about…what happened between us, do they?'

Rick shook his head. 'No, they were discussing the fact that you met someone and he invited you to dinner, but you turned him down.'

'That was Mark Kirkland.' Some colour returned to her cheeks. 'Thank heavens the gossips don't know about…us. They'd have had a field day.'

'It would be a nine-day wonder at most,' Rick said easily. 'Mark Kirkland? Was he the guy at the speed dating who ticked your box?'

For a moment she was transported back to that morning in bed with Rick when she'd received that text from the agency and they had giggled and wrestled over her mobile phone before succumbing to more tender emotions…

She looked across and met his eyes and tried very hard to shut her mind to those memories. 'Why are you asking all these questions, Rick?'

'Because I'm interested,' Rick said nonchalantly, holding her eyes steadily with his. 'So you didn't go out with him?'

'No, I didn't, and just for the record that wasn't because I'm still hankering after my ex-husband. The simple truth is that I've been too busy and too tired to go out on a date with him.'

'And you always put work first,' Rick remarked wryly. 'I noticed that when I was in London. You're first into the office in the morning and last to leave. Have you always been like that or is it just since your divorce?'

'Shall I lie down on a couch so you can analyse me properly?' she countered wryly.

He laughed at that. 'You can if you want, Lucy, but I can't promise I won't get sidetracked.'

She blushed wildly at the husky inflexion behind his words and he smiled. 'Sorry. I shouldn't tease you, should I?'

'No. After what's happened between us I don't think it's appropriate,' she murmured. Then quickly she tried to move the conversation along. 'I can't believe people are still gossiping about my private life. It's been over a year now since my divorce and they still seem fixated by it.'

'Maybe because you and your ex still look as if you are an item.'

'No, we don't! We have to work together, so Kris talks to me and we are civilised about things, but we are definitely not an item.' Lucy's eyes sparkled angrily. 'In fact, I think his girlfriend is pregnant…and before you jump to the conclusion that he's confiding in me, he's not. That was just another little thing I heard on the gossip grapevine recently. In fact I'm surprised that juicy little titbit hasn't reached your ears as well.'

'No, I hadn't heard that.' Rick picked up the bottle of wine and leaned across to top up her glass. 'Was that the news that upset you the night that you met me at Cleary's?'

Lucy flushed hotly. She had forgotten that, in a moment of weakness, she had used that as an excuse for what had happened between them. For a moment she considered lying, saying no, that was some different news…but then she shrugged. What was the point? 'Yes, okay, that was the news. But it didn't upset me in the way you think,' she murmured and darted a defiant glance across the table at him.

'So, in what way did it upset you?'

'It just made me angry, that's all.' Why was he persisting with this, she wondered angrily. 'But that doesn't mean I'm still in love with Kris.' She flashed him a very eloquent look from her emerald-green eyes. 'In fact, I don't even know if I believe in that emotion any more.'

Rick held her gaze steadily and there was silence between them for a heartbeat.

'I've rebuilt my life since Kris walked out. I'm enjoying my work and my life and, contrary to popular belief, I am certainly not pining away for him, or falling apart at the seams.' She raised her head in that determinedly proud way he was starting to recognise. 'And what's more,' she continued firmly, 'I'm stronger since my divorce and I know that no one will ever make me feel the way Kris did ever again.'

Before he could answer her she pushed her chair back from the table. 'Now, if you'll excuse me, I've lost my appetite and I'm very tired, so I think I'll turn in.'

'Lucy—'

She heard him call her name as she walked away across the restaurant, but she didn't look back. Her heart was drumming in her ears and she was furious with herself for losing her cool like that. But she couldn't have sat opposite him for one more minute, or she might have burst into tears.

She had only just reached the sanctuary of her cabin when Rick knocked on the door behind her.

'Lucy?'

'Just go away, Rick. I'll talk to you in the morning.'

'I want to talk to you now,' he said firmly.

Lucy raked a hand through her hair. She was nervous about opening the door because for some reason she felt very emotional. Maybe she was just overtired...

'Lucy, please open the door.'

The gentle tone of his voice was her undoing. Cautiously she moved to do as he asked.

'Hi.' He smiled at her and his eyes moved over the pallor of her skin with concern. 'I'm sorry. I really didn't mean to upset you like that.'

'I think I'm just tired.' She shrugged self-consciously.

'And I get so fed up and angry because the gossip-mongers never seem to leave me alone.'

'I can understand that.' He reached out and stroked a stray strand of her hair back from her face. The gesture was curiously tender and the touch of his hand made her heart flip wildly.

'All I can say, Lucy, is that your ex-husband must be a complete fool.'

'Why would you think that?' She frowned.

'Because he left you.' Rick said the words gently and something about the way he was looking at her, about the tone of his voice, made her ache inside with a strange kind of emotion.

She looked away from him and swallowed the feeling down. Rick was being kind; that was all. 'Thanks, for the vote of confidence.' She smiled and then flicked a look of amusement over at him. 'But he's not that stupid. Sandra is a very beautiful twenty-three-year-old blonde with a figure to die for.'

'But she's not *you*, is she?' Rick said with a shrug.

'I think that was the attraction.' Lucy laughed shakily.

Rick smiled back at her. 'I still think the guy is a fool. And just for the record...' he lowered his voice huskily '...she can't possibly have a lovelier figure than you.'

He's just being charming, she told herself firmly. Don't let it affect you...and definitely don't believe him!

'Rick, don't,' she whispered softly.

'Don't what?' He stepped a little closer.

'Don't try and bamboozle me. All that Latin charisma probably works on every other woman, but it doesn't work on me.' Even as she was speaking she knew she was lying. His charm definitely was working and as she looked into the intense darkness of his eyes she could feel desire twisting inside her like a serpent.

'I'm not trying to bamboozle you.' He smiled as if she

were the most amusing person. 'I admire you and respect you too much for that.'

'Rick, really…don't…' She swallowed down a feeling of complete panic as she felt her resistance starting to fade.

'I mean it, Lucy. I wouldn't hurt you for the world. In fact I'd like to punch anyone who tried to hurt you into the middle of next week, and that includes Kris Bradshaw.'

She smiled shakily at that.

'That's better. You have a beautiful smile, you know.'

'You're doing it again, Rick,' she whispered. 'Don't try and smooth-talk me, because I'm not going to be taken in by it…'

'Didn't anyone ever tell you that you should accept a compliment gracefully?' he said light-heartedly.

'My mother, I think.' She shrugged and then grinned shakily at him. 'But she also said to beware of wolves in sheep's clothing.'

'Your mother is a very wise woman, by the sounds of it.' Rick smiled. 'But I promise I'm not a wolf.'

'Oh, yes, you are,' Lucy murmured.

'Lucy, just accept it…you are a very beautiful, utterly beguiling woman. In fact…' he traced a finger down the side of her face and then tipped her chin upwards so that she was forced to look at him '…ever since we made love I've wanted to do it again.' He reached closer and his lips found hers in a gently provocative kiss. 'And again, and again…'

Each word was punctuated by the most blissfully mind-blowing kiss. And suddenly she was swaying closer and allowing him to do exactly what he wanted.

CHAPTER TEN

SHE'D let it happen again!

As soon as Lucy opened her eyes the thought whipped through her mind with sickening clarity. After all her strong words, all her resolve…here she was again. She turned her head and looked across at the man sleeping next to her.

How had this happened? How was it that Rick only had to lay a hand on her and she was his? For a moment she remembered the sure touch of his hands against her naked skin, the heat of his kisses and the weakness of her body as she had given herself up to the sheer pleasure of his love-making. She remembered the way she had allowed him to undress her and the powerful feeling of arousal and the need that had almost consumed her.

What on earth was the matter with her? He was her boss, for heaven's sake!

Suddenly he opened his eyes and she found herself held by his dark, sexy gaze as they lay looking across the pillow at each other. 'Good morning.' He smiled sleepily at her.

She smiled back, but it was a shadowy smile at best.

'How did you sleep?' he asked with a yawn.

'Okay.' A picture of their naked bodies entwined as Rick brought her very skilfully to climax rushed through her mind. He had sated her and exhausted her completely so that afterwards she had fallen immediately into a deep sleep and she hadn't woken or stirred all night.

He leaned up on his elbow and looked down at her, taking in the luxuriant gloss of her dark hair and the pale luminosity of her skin. 'You look very lovely first thing in the morning, do you know that?' He trailed a hand down the side of her face and the butterfly-light caress made her tingle all over.

'You are one smooth operator, Rick Connors,' she murmured, pulling away from him. 'You know, I told myself that I wasn't going to sleep with you again. I can't believe that I've let myself fall back into bed with you.'

'Well, I'm glad you did.' He leaned a little closer and kissed her on the tip of her nose. 'Very glad, in fact.'

His closeness unnerved her because it sent all sorts of conflicting emotions racing through her. Part of her wanted to carry on where they had left off last night, cuddle close, kiss him and just surrender to the power he had over her senses. The other part of her wanted to run as far away from him as it was possible to get.

Her eyes shimmered over-bright as she looked up at him. 'Yes, but it was a mistake. A big, big mistake,' she told him emphatically.

'Why?'

The calmness of his tone made her blood race angrily. 'Because you're my boss, of course!'

Rick glanced at his wrist-watch. 'Lucy, it's six-thirty in the morning. I'm only your boss during office hours. So relax. I won't ask you to, er, take anything down after eight-thirty, okay?'

The gently teasing tone did nothing to diminish the tension inside her. 'No, it's not okay, Rick. We have to work together. I shouldn't have slept with you. I was weak…overtired. It won't happen again.' She said the words firmly and made to pull away from him, but he caught her before she could move an inch and pulled her gently back.

'But it will happen again, Lucy,' he murmured. 'Because there is a certain chemistry between us. You know it and so do I.'

As if to demonstrate the point, his hand stroked lightly

up over the smooth curve of her waist and instantly she felt her body respond to his touch with a fiery thrust of need.

'So what are you saying?' she murmured huskily. 'That we should just give in to this…this chemistry, or whatever it is?'

'Yes, I suppose I am saying that.' He leaned closer and kissed the side of her face, then nuzzled kisses down her neck. The feeling he generated inside her was one of shivery sweet pleasure. 'We should let this run its course…not think too deeply…just feel the pleasure and enjoy each other…'

For a moment she gave herself up to the blissfully sensuous feelings and allowed herself to turn and meet his lips in a kiss that was explosively passionate.

'See?' He raised his head and looked down into her eyes. 'It's just chemistry. We can make it a no-strings affair— nothing to worry about, nothing to run away from.'

For a second she wanted to agree with him. Maybe he was right; they could have an affair. No big deal; she shouldn't be so old-fashioned. This was just sex. Then as she looked into his eyes she felt a jolt of pure panic as common sense seemed to kick in. She could get badly burnt here.

'No, Rick, this is craziness.' She pulled firmly away from him. 'I don't want any complications in my life and an affair with my boss is one hell of a complication. Last night was a one-off.'

'Can't have been.' He grinned at her wryly. 'Because we've done it before.'

'Don't get smart with me, Rick…' she warned him shakily.

He laughed and reached down and kissed her firmly and possessively on the lips. 'Okay, if it makes you happy, it was a one-off…until next time.'

She frowned. 'There won't be a next time.' She watched as he swung himself out of the bed and her eyes flicked down over his naked body. He really did have a tremendous physique…those broad shoulders tapering down to a taut, powerfully muscled stomach…

Rick glanced over and caught her watching him. He smiled and swiftly she tore her eyes away from him, blushing wildly.

'It will never, ever happen again,' she reiterated fiercely.

Rick laughed and picked up his clothes from the floor. 'Stop fighting it, Lucy. I'll meet you up on deck for breakfast in about thirty minutes, okay? And we'll talk.'

When she didn't answer him immediately he leaned down and planted another swift kiss on her lips. 'Don't be late…'

The door closed behind him. Her heart was thundering against her chest, her blood was zinging through her veins and all kinds of emotions were running wild. Sleeping with him had definitely been a mistake, she told herself angrily, because for one thing the guy was far too sure of himself, far too arrogantly confident. *Good in bed, though…* The thought crept in unwanted. He was extremely passionate and tender. She liked the way he whispered things to her in the darkness, things about how good she felt, how much he wanted her… Just remembering made her stomach flip. Maybe he was right; maybe they should just give into this. The chemistry between them was strong; maybe they should just let it run its course and after a short time it would burn itself out.

Feeling totally confused, she swung her legs out of bed and headed off to have a shower. A relationship just based on sex didn't seem right somehow. She wasn't sure she could handle it.

It was as she turned on the hot water in the shower that she felt suddenly sick. The nausea was accompanied by a severe feeling of debilitation and all she could do was lean against the washbasin taking deep steadying breaths. She didn't know if she was going to be sick or whether she was going to pass out. It was a horrible feeling and she couldn't move for several moments, then thankfully, as suddenly as the illness came, it seemed to pass.

What on earth had caused that? she wondered, staring at herself in the mirror. She looked very pale and drawn. Maybe it was the heat in here; her reflection was starting to steam up now. Hastily she flicked on the cold water and rinsed her face. Then she turned down the heat of the shower and stepped beneath a cooling jet. The sensation was refreshing and by the time she had dressed in a pair of lightweight white linen trousers and a black and white T-shirt she was looking remarkably well again.

It was probably nothing, she told herself as she headed towards the lifts. More worrying was what she should say to Rick over breakfast—how she should handle things between them.

Considering the fact that it was so early in the morning, the heat out on deck was incredible. There was a dazzling blue sky and the sea was a clear turquoise. There was no sign of Rick in the restaurant, but the table they had sat at last night was set up for breakfast under the shade of a giant green parasol. A waiter appeared, pulled out a chair for her and handed her a menu, and a few minutes later Rick sauntered in from the opposite direction.

He was wearing a pair of khaki-coloured trousers and a beige T-shirt. His hair was still damp from a shower. He looked fresh and vital and intensely attractive.

'Sorry, I got held up on the phone.' To her surprise he leaned down and kissed her on the cheek. The scent of his cologne was delicious, as was the brief moment of intimacy, much to her consternation. She flicked a glance around the restaurant to see if any of the staff had witnessed the kiss.

'Relax, Lucy.' Rick grinned at her as he took his seat opposite. 'There's nobody here and I assure you no member of the paparazzi is going to pop up from behind a potted plant.'

'Very funny, Rick, but if word of us gets back to the office I'll never hear the end of it.'

Rick nodded. 'I understand your concerns. And, to be honest, I'm wary mixing business with pleasure myself.'

Did that mean he had changed his mind about wanting to take her to bed again? She felt a momentary pang of disappointment and was immediately annoyed with herself. 'So we're both agreed, then, that the best thing would be if we could try to forget all about this,' she said firmly.

'And do you think that if you say it in a determined enough voice we'll just be able to do that?'

The sardonic tone made her blush.

'Lucy, as I said to you this morning, the chemistry is there; we may as well just face it. And just because you were my mistress, it wouldn't mean we couldn't have a good working relationship. Both of us are business orientated. Neither of us is looking for a long-term commitment; we both know the score.'

'I see.' Lucy felt her heart thump against her chest. 'You sound as if you've got this all worked out.'

'I wouldn't go that far.' He smiled at her. 'But, yes, I'd like you to take the job here in Barbados. I reckon it will take the best part of a year to get the office established. And during that time we could have some fun together.'

'And during that year the chemistry between us will have subsided.' She looked across at him, hardly able to believe that they were having this conversation. 'Is that what you're thinking?'

'I think we should just take things a day at a time,' Rick said gently.

'Well, I suppose that's easy for you to say,' Lucy said pointedly. 'When the affair ends you won't be the one worrying about your job.'

'You think if we stop sleeping together that I'll fire you?' Rick's tone was sharp for a moment. 'I thought we'd progressed past the point where you thought I was a ruthless bastard.'

'We have,' Lucy murmured awkwardly. 'I don't think that about you.' She looked across at him and their eyes met. 'But I can't help wondering now if you've offered me the job out here because you want me in your bed.'

'Lucy, I'm a businessman first and foremost.' Rick shook his head. 'There is no way I'd have offered you such a responsible job if I didn't think you were the best person for it. There is a lot of money riding on this new venture of mine and it's too important for me to jeopardise it in any way.'

She felt rather foolish now for asking the question. The waiter arrived and asked if they'd like tea or coffee. They both asked for coffee and watched silently as he poured them a cup then put the pot down on the table between them.

'Are you ready to order now?' the waiter asked as he stepped back.

'I'll just have some toast, please,' Lucy said without looking at the menu.

'Is that all you want?' Rick frowned across at her. 'You didn't eat anything last night. You must be hungry.'

'Really, I'm fine with just toast. I don't normally eat any breakfast.' She smiled at the waiter and handed him the menu back.

Rick ordered some maple syrup pancakes. Lucy's stomach protested just at the thought. In fact, even the smell of the coffee was upsetting her somewhat. Maybe it was the heat; maybe nerves from their discussion. She pushed the cup away and reached to pour herself a glass of water.

'Are you okay?' Rick asked her as the waiter left them. 'You look a bit pale.'

'That's the effect of the English climate.' She smiled

across at him. 'Hopefully I'll look a bit better by the end of the day.'

'You always look beautiful,' Rick said softly. He glanced across at her and met her eyes steadily. 'So what do you say—shall we give an affair a whirl? See where it leads us?'

The words were so casual, yet the way he was looking at her was anything but. She felt her heart thump painfully against her chest. There was a part of her that wanted to throw caution to the wind and just say yes. In one way it sounded exciting…in another it sounded dangerous.

'I'll think about it, Rick,' she murmured. 'Apart from anything else, I haven't decided yet whether or not I'm going to take the job you've offered me out here. And I suppose one thing is dependent on the other. I can't very well be your mistress if I'm in London and you're here.' She tried very hard to sound as casual about things as he did.

'Fair enough.' He nodded. 'But just one thing: even if you decide you don't want to continue with our relationship, I still want you to consider the job here.'

'Don't worry. Like you, I always put work first.' She took a sip of her water, and then glanced across at him wryly. What made him tick? she wondered. What drove him?

Business was obviously his main concern, the most important mistress in his life. She supposed he hadn't got where he was without being single-minded in his dealings. The business reports she had read on EC Cruises had all confirmed that.

'You are looking at me very pensively,' Rick said suddenly.

'Am I?' She blushed. 'I was just thinking how little I know about you. And yet here we are sitting over breakfast talking very casually about having an affair.'

'You know that sexually we are very compatible,' he said huskily.

She tried very hard not to look embarrassed. 'And that

your heart was broken at the age of seven by Marion Woods,' she said lightly.

He laughed at that. 'You see, you know more about me than most women. I don't think I've ever told anyone about Marion Woods before.'

The waiter arrived with their food. Lucy wondered if she should leave the conversation there. She sensed that Rick was a very private person, that he didn't really like it when she asked him too many in-depth questions.

But as they were left alone again she realised she didn't want to leave the conversation. She wanted to know more about him.

'Did you grow up in Buenos Aires?' she asked curiously.

'I was there until the age of seven, and then I was sent to boarding-school in England.'

'It must have been tough leaving your parents at such a young age.'

'It was okay. The tough part was four years later when they got divorced. All hell seemed to break loose. My father moved to live in London, my mother went with her new boyfriend to live in Miami. So holidays had to be split between the two.'

'That must have been difficult,' Lucy said sympathetically. 'Did you have any brothers or sisters?'

'I have a stepsister, from my mother's second marriage. And yes, it was a difficult time. My parents' divorce was very acrimonious and some twelve years later the fallout was still ongoing. The family business, which had been a very successful chain of restaurants, almost went into receivership because of it.' Rick reached to pour himself another coffee. 'My first job after leaving university was to go in to try and salvage things. You could say I was thrown in at the deep end.'

'And did you salvage it?' Lucy glanced across at Rick, watching the way the warm breeze ruffled his dark hair.

'Eventually, but it took a few years.' He glanced across at her and smiled. 'You ask a lot of questions.'

'Not as many as you asked me last night,' she said pointedly.

He laughed at that. *'Touché.'*

'And anyway,' she continued resolutely, 'if I'm going to become your mistress I need to know a little more about you.'

'I see.' Rick smiled over at her. It was an indulgent kind of smile and for some reason it made her heart rate speed up, made her almost forget what she was saying.

'Well, go ahead, then,' he encouraged her with a grin.

'So…how did you go from there to owning a chain of hotels and EC Cruises?'

'Once the restaurants were on their feet I split them up, sold half and turned the rest into franchises. From there we bought other businesses; some I split and sold off in smaller pieces, some I kept.'

'So you were an asset-stripper,' Lucy said dryly.

'I did what had to be done to turn a profit.' Rick shrugged. For a moment she had a glimpse of steely determination in his eyes. 'My father asked me to turn his company around for him and that's what I did. Along the way I made money for myself as well as him. I'm a businessman.'

'And are you still working with your father?'

'Since he told me about his health problems last year I've stepped in from time to time to try and keep an eye on things for him. But I'm pretty much tied up with my own company. So I'm trying to arrange for one of my managers, Karina Stockwell, to go in to oversee things for him.'

'Karina?' Lucy glanced across at him as the name resonated inside her. Was that the woman who had been waiting for Rick at the London office, the woman with the husky, sexy voice? She hardly liked to ask that question.

'Have I told you about Karina before?' Rick frowned.

'Was she in London just before you flew to New York?' Rick nodded. 'Karina and I go way back. We lived together for a few years.'

'She's the woman your father wanted you to marry?'

'Yes, that's right. My father was very fond of Karina. Still is. But I think that's just his business head talking.'

'So what happened between you two?' Lucy tried to sound casual.

'It just didn't work out. We cared about each other—still do, and we are still good friends. But the relationship had run its course.'

'Who decided to call it a day?' She probably shouldn't have asked that question, but she couldn't help herself. There was a heartbeat of a second before he answered her.

'It was a mutual decision.' Rick looked across at her wryly. 'I'm not pretending that I've been an angel where women are concerned, Lucy. I know I haven't been. I've had a lot of girlfriends, probably broken a few hearts... unintentionally, of course.' He met her eyes firmly.

'But of course.' She echoed his words sardonically. 'Because you didn't really mean to stand them up, it was just that there was an important office meeting, or there was a crisis on the factory floor, et cetera, et cetera.'

'Okay.' Rick shrugged. 'Work has always come first. But I've always tried to be honest with people and told them that up front.'

'And did you tell Karina that up front or was she different?'

There was a moment's silence. 'Yes, Karina was different.' He leaned back in his chair and for just a moment she wondered if she glimpsed a flicker of regret in his eyes. 'And I was serious about her. But I knew marriage wouldn't work for us.'

'She wanted a family man, not a workaholic,' Lucy guessed.

'It wasn't quite that black and white,' Rick said curtly.

'Sorry.' She glanced away from him. 'I shouldn't have said that. It was far too personal.'

'Karina and I have managed to remain good friends. And she's married now. So, you see, some things happen for a reason. They are meant to be.'

'I suppose they are.'

She wondered suddenly if his aversion towards marriage was based on his experience of his parents' divorce.

Their eyes met across the table and there was a moment's silence.

'So, is the interview terminated?' He asked the question flippantly.

'Just about.' She smiled.

'And do I pass?' His voice was still laced with amusement.

'Just about.'

'Good, because I think we've done enough talking.' He reached across the table and took hold of her hand. 'We've got until three this afternoon before everyone arrives for the cruise. So how about I show you around the new offices...and take you out to the place I've earmarked especially for you?'

'Earmarked?' The touch of his fingers stroking against hers was sending bizarre little electrical impulses shooting through her. The feeling made her hot inside; made her want to move closer, feel his hands more intimately on her body. 'Earmarked for what?'

'For you to live, of course.'

'Oh. You've already found somewhere?'

'Yes.' He let go of her and stood up from the table. 'Come on, I'll show you.'

As Lucy sat beside him in his car she thought that she

would always remember this day in her mind. Everything looked so clear and freshly vital, the intense blue of the sky, the beauty of Barbados with its green fields and white beaches fringed with turquoise water.

Rick put the top down on his car and they roared along narrow lanes through the centre of the island, past whispering fields of sugar cane and small churches that looked as if they had been transported straight from a Devon English village into a tropical setting of palm trees and bougainvillea.

At the crest of a hill Rick slowed the car and below them Lucy could see a spectacular coastline where the Atlantic crashed in against deserted white beaches fringed by palm trees and fields of sugar cane.

'Beautiful, isn't it?' he said, looking over at her with a smile.

She nodded. 'It's breathtaking.'

'My house is just over there.' He pointed to a road leading off to the left and she could just make out a large manortype house almost hidden by trees. 'You can't see it very well from here.' He put the car in gear and set off down the road again and a few minutes later turned through some high gateposts to pull up outside a quaint wooden house on stilts with a wraparound veranda. It was painted a pretty primrose-yellow and was surrounded by a riot of tropical greenery, lemon and banana trees, avocado and papaya.

'Here we are.' He turned the engine off. 'I thought you would like it here.'

Lucy glanced up at the house, totally charmed by it. 'This is for me?'

'If you like it.' Rick opened the car door and stepped out. 'Come on, I'll show you around.'

Hesitantly Lucy followed him. How anyone could not like this house, she didn't know. The property was like something from a tropical painting by Gauguin, delightfully proportioned and full of character. The first thing that struck her was the view from the veranda down towards the sea and the delicious warm breeze that rustled through the trees. There was no sound except the waves breaking on the beach and the occasional bird call.

Rick unlocked the front door and they walked straight into a living room with polished wooden floors and windows that folded back to allow the breeze to circulate through the building. It was furnished with the most exquisite taste. Polished mahogany tables and a desk positioned to look out towards the sea, a sofa and chairs in the palest of yellow damask.

Rick opened the door off it and there was a dining room with a large hardwood table and six carving chairs. Patio doors led out to the veranda.

Next to that was a large white kitchen with black granite counters and every modern convenience.

Lucy wandered silently from room to room.

Rick opened one of the doors and she found herself in a room with floor-to-ceiling windows that looked down towards the sea.

'I always think this room would make a good artist's studio,' Rick said nonchalantly. 'If you moved here maybe you'd take up your painting again?'

Lucy smiled at him. 'And maybe turn into the new Picasso?'

Rick laughed at that. She liked the sound of his laugh; it sounded warm and enticing. She wondered what it would be like to live in this house...and how often Rick would visit her. The question made strange little butterflies dance in her stomach. Hastily she stepped away from him out into the corridor again.

The room next door was the master bedroom. It held an enormous four-poster bed that was swathed in white nets and it looked tropically inviting...very seductive. Lucy tried to quickly step back out of the room, but Rick was behind her now in the open doorway.

'So what do you think?' he asked quietly. 'Do you like the house?'

'It would be hard not to like it.' She pretended to be absorbed in looking out of the windows at the sea. 'Does it belong to you?'

'Yes. It's the gatehouse. I live about a fifteen-minute walk away.'

'I see.' Her heart thumped crazily against her chest. So it wasn't far for him to visit.

'I know you are very independent and also that you're concerned about people gossiping about us, so I thought if you had this house it might just waylay a few of your concerns.'

'So I'd be your secret mistress?' She tried to make a joke, but her voice wavered unsteadily. She felt completely out of her depth. Rick took hold of her arm and pulled her around to face him.

'That's up to you,' he said quietly and his eyes held hers with a penetrating intensity that made her go hot inside. 'Personally I'd like everyone to know that your nights belong to me.' He reached out and traced a whisper soft caress over the side of her face. 'That you belong to me...'

A shiver of desire stirred powerfully inside her.

His eyes were on her lips now and she felt herself starting to sway closer to him. Drawn, trapped by an irresistible force that was telling her she needed to belong to him...that she would willingly give herself, do anything, just to be his.

Rick's lips touched hers with a commanding force that seemed to shake her inside. She rested her arms against him and kissed him back. For a while all confusion was lost in a whirl of pleasure and passion.

She felt his hand moving under her T-shirt, stroking her breast through the lace of her bra. Immediately her body responded to him and an ache of need opened wide inside her.

'I want you, Lucy.' He whispered the words against her ear and her heart slammed unsteadily against her chest. 'I want you right here, right now and on a very…very regular basis…'

The slam of a door somewhere in the house broke the sensual spell and hastily she pulled back from him, rearranging her T-shirt with fumbling hands, her face burning with embarrassment.

'Hello, Mr Connors,' a cheerful voice called from the lounge. 'Only me.'

'Relax, Lucy.' Rick smiled wryly. 'It's Mrs Lawson, my cleaner. I asked her to make the place ready for you, for when you return from the cruise.' Rick moved towards the door. 'I'll ask her to come back later.'

'No!' Lucy stopped him quickly. 'Don't, Rick.'

He turned and looked at her with questioning eyes.

'I don't want to fall into bed with you here. I need more time to think about things.' She said the words huskily. 'This is all moving too fast.'

'On the contrary, I don't think it's moving fast enough.' Rick smiled wryly. 'But then, patience never was one of my virtues. When I make my mind up about something I don't usually like waiting around.'

'Well, you'll have to wait, Rick,' she said firmly, and there was a determined gleam in her eyes as she looked over at him now. 'Obviously you've had time to give this…situation some thought, but don't forget you've only just sprung the idea on me. And maybe other women in your life have been quick to fall in with your plans at a moment's notice, but I'm different.'

'Oh, I realise that, Lucy,' he said and his smile broadened, his eyes gleaming with amusement. 'I got the drift of that the moment I first set eyes on you.'

'Good.' Her voice was calm and decisive. 'Then you should realise that the best thing you can do now is give me space and time to think about this. In fact I don't think you should…kiss me, or…or come near me until I've made my mind up about things, because it will only confuse matters.'

'You think?' Rick's voice was dry and the amusement still flickered in the depths of his dark eyes.

'Yes, I do.' She held his gaze resolutely, but as she looked across at him she knew that he was all too aware of the fact that all he had to do was walk across, take her into his arms and all her cool, logical resolutions would be thrown to the wind.

For a few seconds there was silence, then to her relief he inclined his head in agreement.

'Okay, Lucy, we'll play things your way…for now.'

CHAPTER ELEVEN

THE ship was preparing to pull out of the harbour. Lucy stood out on deck and watched the activity on the quay below. The last of the ropes were being released and the engines were stirring the water up into a white froth as the *Contessa* slipped her moorings and pushed away from the land.

With that suddenness of the Tropics the sun was sinking and the sky was streaked with orange and purple light. It reflected over the darkness of the water and lit the island of Barbados in the purple misty haze of twilight.

A few people on the dockside waved and Lucy waved back. Then the ship gave two loud blasts on its horn and turned for the open sea leaving a wake of white froth. Lucy was the only person out on the deck. She guessed that everyone was down in their cabins getting ready for the captain's cocktail party before dinner and she didn't know where Rick was. She hadn't seen him since his guests had arrived this afternoon.

Lucy had got ready early. She was wearing a long black dress with shoestring straps and her long hair was carefully swept upwards and held in place with some diamanté clips. With time to spare she watched as the sun disappeared completely and the lights on Barbados twinkled in the darkness.

Her mind played back over the day. After taking her to the gatehouse, Rick had called briefly at his own house to pick up his luggage. She had drunk a glass of ice tea in one of the formal reception rooms as she had waited for him, and had wandered around admiring the style and grandeur of his house. Until then she hadn't really thought a great deal about how wealthy Rick was. But that house must have been worth a fortune. It was palatial, with its numerous rooms and terraces and two large swimming pools. Lucy thought that her flat would probably have fitted into just one of the downstairs rooms and the furnishings alone must have cost a fortune.

It made her realise how different she was from Rick—how in fact they inhabited different worlds altogether. She was just an ordinary career girl with overheads that she sometimes worried about. Rick lived in a mansion with a team of staff and was used to the best of everything. Not that she was overly impressed with all that luxury—in fact, of the two houses today she probably would have chosen the gatehouse as a home anyway, not Rick's mansion—and as for the staff, she was probably too independent for all that help.

Barbados was fading into the distance now and the bright blanket of stars overhead and just the faintest twinkle of light from the coast were all that lit the tropical night.

Lucy wondered what it would be like to live on that island. Having a mansion and lots of money wouldn't excite her, but having Rick—lying in his arms…now, that set her senses reeling with a very different kind of excitement. She imagined her belongings in the gatehouse; imagined sitting out on the terrace in the heat of the evening, having a drink with him. Imagined him taking her by the hand and leading her into that cool white bedroom…

Swiftly she turned her mind away from that. Okay, she knew that they were sexually compatible, but there were more important things to think about than that.

After Rick had taken her to his house they had gone to visit the new offices down by the docks. They were large and modern and just a few minutes' walk from the capital. In practical terms she thought she would enjoy working there and would relish the new challenge of setting the business up.

So why was she hesitating about saying yes to Rick? she wondered in confusion.

She wanted him—heavens, she wanted him so much she could feel her stomach twisting with an ache of longing— and yet she was scared.

What she was scared of, she had no idea…maybe of being hurt again?

But Rick couldn't hurt her, she told herself firmly, not in the way Kris had hurt her anyway, because she didn't love him. She would never, ever let her heart be captured and broken like that again.

Lucy turned and looked along the deserted deck. Through the windows of the cocktail bar she could see the band were setting up for their evening performance. In a little while everyone would be arriving and she would have to be by Rick's side to help with some of the introductions. She was about to head back down to her cabin to pick up her handbag and have a last-minute check through the guest-list when she saw Rick walking into the bar.

He looked magnificent in his dark dress suit. Tall and handsome, he made her heart skip wildly. In fact she was so immersed in him that she didn't notice for a moment the woman on his arm. It was only when she reached up and whispered something close to his ear that Lucy's attention transferred to her. Rick laughed and as Lucy watched he put a hand under her chin and tipped her face up to look into her eyes.

For a moment the picture seemed to freeze in Lucy's mind. They made a very attractive couple. The woman was wearing a long red dress and was tall and willowy with short blonde hair. Lucy couldn't see her features properly, but from a distance she was stunning, like a supermodel.

Rick said something to her, then they went to sit down

in an alcove by the bar. Who was that woman? And was it her imagination or was there something intensely personal about the moment she had just witnessed? Obviously the two had arranged to meet early, before the crowds descended.

Lucy frowned as a sudden thought struck her. Was that Karina? She knew the other woman was a manager and most of the upper echelons of management were on board. So it stood to sense that she would be here. She wished she could go down and check on her list, but Rick had only given her the names from her side of the company.

Annoyed with herself for caring, she made her way back down to her cabin. So what if it was Karina? The two were good friends; they were probably just catching up with each other.

Lucy sat at the dressing table in her cabin and reapplied some gloss to her lips. Then she brushed some more blusher over her cheeks. Despite the sunshine today, she still looked pale.

The downside of being Rick's mistress would be that she would never be sure of him. The thought crept into her consciousness. There would always be other women in the background waiting, watching. With his looks and money it was inevitable.

Could she live like that? She knew Mel would tell her not to be so serious, to get with the modern programme. She could almost hear her friend's voice. 'Well, if he goes out with someone else, so can you. Just enjoy yourself.'

But Lucy didn't want to go out with anybody else and she certainly didn't like to think of Rick doing so. Even the thought of him being upstairs alone with his ex was eating into her. She remembered the way he had looked at the other woman, touched her, and something twisted inside her like a snake. She was jealous!

Lucy slammed the make-up brush down and glared at

herself in the mirror. Now she was being pathetic! Of course she wasn't jealous. She didn't care.

But the words rang hollowly inside her. She did care…in fact, she cared more than she could ever remember caring about anyone before. She was in love with Rick Connors.

The knowledge rushed in from nowhere and ricocheted painfully inside her, and for a moment she sat there in total shock. It couldn't be true, it just couldn't. She hardly knew the man, she told herself fiercely. And he wasn't even trustworthy…look how he had even lied to her about who he was! Desperately she searched around for all the reasons why her heart shouldn't get involved with him. He was probably a womaniser; he was too rich and probably too ambitious in business… But no matter what excuses she dragged up, her heart still thumped painfully with the realisation that it didn't matter how many sensible words she threw at herself. Her heart had made its decision. It had chosen Rick.

She had never felt this strongly about any man before, she realised shakily. Not even Kris, and look how he had hurt her! If Kris could hurt her like that, what could Rick do to her?

For a moment Lucy felt sick, she was so appalled…so frightened. After all her strong words about not getting involved with someone again, she had chosen a total heartbreaker and given her emotions to him on a plate.

But it wasn't too late, she told herself shakily. She would have to be strong and back away from the situation, say no to his proposition. Because she couldn't be his mistress, not now, knowing what she did. It would destroy her emotionally.

She would get over this. She was strong, and she would prove it by giving Rick her decision this very evening. And she would turn down his job here as well. She couldn't risk being near him.

Snatching up her handbag, she headed out of her cabin into the lounge and walked straight into Rick on the other side of the door.

'Hey, where are you tearing off to in such a hurry?' He put a steadying hand on her shoulder.

'I...I just didn't want to be late.' The light touch of his hand against her bare skin triggered an immediate response from her body and made her acutely conscious once more of just how easily he could stir desire in her. Quickly she took a step back.

'Well, you don't need to dash around like that. There's plenty of time.' He smiled at her. And even his smile set her senses reeling.

How blind she had been, she thought hazily. She had fallen for him almost from the first moment their eyes had met. And she had been so busy fighting it and making excuses for it that she hadn't seen the danger she was in, until now. And now it felt far, far too late. How could she end things feeling as she did? How could she tell him she never wanted to see him again? The very thought was like a knife in her heart. Suddenly all her strong resolutions were hanging precariously by a thread.

'We've got a few minutes to spare,' he said gently.

A few minutes for what? she wondered, and felt her temperature starting to increase as she noticed the way his eyes swept over her appreciatively.

'You look extremely beautiful,' he told her huskily.

Her emotions turned over. 'Thank you.' She whispered the words.

'I like your hair up like that. It makes you look very sophisticated.' His eyes moved from her hairstyle down over her naked shoulder and the low sweep of her dress over creamy skin.

She wished he wouldn't look at her so closely. She could

feel herself starting to tingle all over. 'Well, I'm glad I pass the test.' She tried to make light of the compliment.

'Oh, you definitely pass the test,' he said with a grin. 'You passed that a while ago. There's just one thing missing…'

'What's that?' She watched as he reached into the top pocket of his jacket and brought out a long narrow box.

'A little something I bought for you in New York.'

She leaned closer to see, but he waved her away. 'It's a necklace. Turn around and I'll put it on for you.'

Taken aback, she did as he asked. 'You really shouldn't be buying me things,' she told him shakily. She closed her eyes as she felt the light touch of his hands against her skin and it set all sorts of fires racing through her body.

'Why shouldn't I buy you something?' he murmured quietly as he deftly fastened the clasp. 'There…let me look at you.'

She turned and his eyes swept over her appraisingly. 'Now that is the perfect finishing touch.'

She should tell him that she couldn't accept the gift, that the affair was over. The words burned inside her, but she couldn't say them. Lucy fingered the heavy necklace tensely and then stepped across to glance at her reflection in the mirror.

The piece of jewellery was fabulous. It was beaten luminous silver with snake-like tentacles curling from a fine filigree band. She noticed as she leaned closer that some of the silver strands had what looked like Aztec writing down the sides. 'This is beautiful, Rick. It's so unusual. But you shouldn't have…'

'Stop saying that, Lucy, I'm just glad you like it. I saw it as I was walking along Fifth Avenue and I immediately thought it would look good on you.' He smiled. 'It's a limited edition copy of a necklace worn by an Aztec princess. Apparently it was given to her by her lover, and the scrolls down along some of the silver tentacles have secret meanings.'

Lucy was intrigued. 'What kind of secret meanings?'

Rick smiled. 'Maybe I should whisper that to you at some later date?' His voice lowered huskily, and he reached out to stroke one hand over her shoulder, tracing the line of the necklace with a casual yet intensely sensual caress.

Lucy wanted to move closer…wanted him to tell her: *now*. She looked up and met the dark, intense look in his eyes and was lost. She couldn't end it. She just couldn't.

Looking down at her, Rick saw the shadows in her eyes. The brief conflict in her was all too apparent. Her ex-husband had certainly done a job of breaking her heart, he thought angrily. Sometimes the wariness he saw in those beautiful eyes made him so angry he wanted to punch the guy. 'Lucy, I'm not going to rush you about things so you don't need to worry.'

'I know…' She shook her head, the gentleness in his tone making her resistance melt further.

'Good.' He smiled at her. 'Well, I suppose we should get up on deck and meet our guests. Did you look over the list I gave you?'

The swift change of tone towards business made her senses whirl with confusion. 'Yes, I looked at it earlier.'

'Okay, well, let's get this show on the road.' He put a guiding hand at her back and together they left the room.

The captain and a few first officers were in the cocktail lounge. Rick introduced her and for a while they stood around making light conversation. Captain Michaels told her that they were due to dock in Grenada, the Spice Island, at six-thirty tomorrow morning.

There was a very convivial atmosphere. The band was playing a medley of swing numbers and waiters were circulating with champagne and canapés. Then the rest of the guests started to arrive and the time seemed to fly by as

Lucy concentrated on social niceties and making sure that everything ran smoothly.

By the time she had shaken hands with the hundredth guest through the doors, and smiled and said the right things to the right people, Lucy could almost have forgotten the fact that she had fallen in love with the one man she shouldn't have, could almost have persuaded herself that the emotions earlier were just a figment of her imagination— and then the doors opened and the woman Lucy had seen earlier walked in.

'Karina, hi.' Rick placed a hand on her arm and kissed her on both cheeks with the laid-back confidence of someone very much at ease.

'Hi again.' She smiled up at him with warmth and sincerity, and even reached up and very proprietorially brushed a stray strand of his hair away from his face.

And suddenly from nowhere all those horrible feelings of jealousy were twisting inside Lucy again.

'Lucy, I'd like you to meet Karina Stockwell. She's my right-hand woman in the day-to-day running of several businesses, and also a very good friend.'

Lucy smiled at the woman and reached to shake her hand. It was utterly ridiculous to be jealous of her, she told herself firmly. Jealousy was an ugly and destructive emotion and she would not give in to it. And, besides, Karina and Rick's close relationship was in the past—the woman was married now.

'Rick's told me all about you,' Karina said cheerily. 'I believe he's hoping you'll front up the new offices in Barbados.'

'That's right.' Lucy felt her smile slipping just a little. Somehow the thought that Rick had been discussing her made her feel uncomfortable. Exactly what had he been saying? She was tempted to say, *Rick's told me about you as well*, but she held her tongue.

A waiter arrived with a tray of drinks. Lucy helped herself to one and looked around towards Rick, but he was talking to someone else now.

'So, are you going to take the job?' Karina asked as she helped herself to a glass.

'I haven't made up my mind yet.' Lucy shrugged.

'Well, speaking from experience, working closely with Rick can be wonderful fun.' Karina took a sip of her champagne. 'Of course, he's a businessman to his fingertips.'

Lucy laughed. 'Yes, I noticed.'

Karina smiled back at her. 'I wish you luck, Lucy.'

Meaning what? Lucy wondered. That she would need it? Before she could answer, the crowds were swirling in around them and the conversation moved on. Then it was time for everyone to move through to the dining room for dinner.

The food was delicious, but Lucy couldn't help wishing that it were just her and Rick sitting out on deck under the stars like last night…only this time she wouldn't waste time talking about her ex-husband.

By contrast tonight they were in the more formal surroundings of the main dining room. Lucy was sitting at a large table opposite Rick. On his left sat Karina, on his right John Layton's wife. There were a few other managers around the table as well and Lucy was between John Layton and the ship's doctor, a rather pleasant middle-aged Scottish man.

The conversation flowed and Rick in particular was extremely entertaining.

Good-looking, amusing, intelligent…the list was endless, she thought as she glanced across the table at him. But she would still have to turn him down, she told herself firmly, because she could get badly burnt here, just like Karina Stockwell.

It was noticeable that Karina hadn't brought her husband

with her on this trip. Most of the other members of staff were accompanied by their partners. Lucy couldn't help wondering if the other woman still held a torch for Rick. She seemed to pay a lot of attention to him, to look very deeply into his eyes when he said anything to her.

John Layton leaned across towards her cutting into her thoughts. 'Before I forget, Lucy, Kris asked me to pass on a message to you.'

'Oh?' She looked around at him in surprise.

'He wants you to ring him.'

Lucy frowned. 'Did he say what it was about?'

John shook his head. 'But he did say it was rather urgent.'

'That's strange.' Lucy shook her head. 'But knowing Kris's sense of the dramatic, it's probably nothing.'

'Maybe he's going to try and tap you up for a job out here,' John suggested with a grin.

'I don't think so.' Lucy smiled at him. 'But you never know. Tell you what, I'll make him sweat for a few days and ring him when I get back to Barbados.'

'Good idea.' John said. 'And whatever it is he wants, Lucy, you tread with care around that man. I wouldn't like to see you hurt again.'

Lucy smiled at John, touched by the sincerity in his tone. 'Don't worry, John, that's not going to happen.'

Lucy glanced across the table. Karina was flirting with Rick now, laughing over some incident that had happened in the office years ago. Her wide blue eyes were trained on him, and one manicured hand rested on his shoulder. Lucy glanced away again and tried to pretend she didn't notice. But suddenly she was remembering another office party years ago, when Kris had sat opposite her and flirted like crazy with a woman who had been working as a temp on the reception. Lucy hadn't let it bother her; she had just told herself that it was a Christmas party and Kris had had too much to drink.

It had been much later in the evening when she had overheard some colleagues having a discussion in the Ladies' about whether she suspected anything or not.

She could still remember that conversation as clearly as if it had happened yesterday. 'Kris really was sailing close to the wind tonight. Do you think she suspects he's having an affair? If she doesn't, she must be blind… And she is always so considerate to him, isn't she, so understanding? Letting him just go on that holiday and believing it was with the boys! Someone should say something to her. He's really taking her for a fool.'

Everyone had known…everyone except her. The memory of that humiliation was still there, buried somewhere deep down inside.

Lucy closed her eyes for just a moment. Why was she thinking about that? she wondered angrily. It was in the past and should be forgotten. When she glanced upwards she found that Rick was watching her.

Their eyes met and he smiled at her and suddenly it was as if everyone else in the restaurant disappeared and there were just the two of them.

Lucy could feel her heart thumping painfully against her ribs. She didn't know what to think where Rick was concerned. One minute she felt she could trust him totally, to the ends of the earth; the next she just wasn't sure if she was being naïve in the extreme. He'd asked her to be his mistress, nothing more.

Hastily she looked away.

The meal was drawing to an end. Lucy refused coffee and as a few people excused themselves from the table she took the opportunity to escape.

Most people were heading through to one of the main lounges to listen to a concert. But Lucy slipped out onto the deck. She felt she needed some fresh air to clear her mind.

The night was warm and balmy and Lucy walked around

towards the front of the ship watching the way she cut through the darkness of the sea. There was a full moon up in the sky and it reflected over the water, lighting it in patches as bright as the necklace Rick had placed around her neck.

Lucy leaned against the balustrade and breathed in the salt air.

'There you are.' Rick's voice from behind her made her turn. 'What are you doing out here?'

'Just admiring the view, and getting some fresh air.'

'It's warmer out here than it is inside.'

'Yes, that takes a bit of getting used to.' She laughed. 'But it's beautiful, isn't it?'

'Yes, it is,' he agreed, coming to stand beside her at the rail.

For a while they stood in silence, watching the ship ploughing steadily through the silky blackness of the sea. It was calm and peaceful, the only sound the gentle surge of water against the bow. 'When you live in the city you forget how beautiful the sky is at night,' Lucy murmured, looking upwards at the myriad stars.

'You can certainly see the stars better out here.' Rick placed a light arm around her shoulder. 'There are the Three Sisters.' He pointed out the constellation. 'And the Plough…'

Lucy could smell the scent of his cologne; it was warm and provocative and made her senses reel in disorder. She allowed herself to lean her head against his shoulder as she looked up. 'Do you think the stars really control our destiny?' she asked him suddenly.

He laughed. 'I think we control our own destiny.'

'Ah, there is an arrogant man talking,' she said with a smile. 'I think there is a far higher power that holds and controls us all.'

'Maybe.' Rick shrugged.

'What star sign are you?' she asked him suddenly.

'Leo.'

'Figures.'

'Now what do you mean by that?' he asked with amusement.

'Bossy, likes to be in charge.'

'Oh, really? So what star sign are you?' He laughed.

'Libra.'

'Now, let me take a guess. Stubborn, likes to do things her way, rather infuriating?'

'Well balanced, actually,' she said with a grin. 'But likes to weigh things up carefully.'

'I definitely noticed that.' Rick turned her around so that she was looking up at him instead of the stars. 'So tell me, how do Leo and Libra get along?'

'I'm not sure.' Her heart started to thump unevenly. 'I think that depends on the alignment of the planets when they were born. And I reckon you were born under the proverbial wandering star.'

'I like travelling, so maybe you have something there. And what about you?' he asked, suddenly serious. 'Do you like travelling to far-flung places or are you a home bird?'

'Depends who I'm with,' she said softly. 'I think people are more important than places.'

'So if you moved to Barbados you'd miss your friends?'

'I suppose so.'

'Would you miss seeing your ex-husband?'

Lucy frowned. 'Why do you keep asking me about him?'

'Because I know you think about him a lot. You were thinking about him tonight, weren't you?'

Rick noticed the way she blushed.

'Only because John Layton mentioned him to me,' she murmured defensively.

'Yes, I heard.' Rick's voice was dry.

'Really?' Lucy was surprised. 'I thought you were too

busy hanging on Karina's every word to hear anything John was saying.' As soon as she said the words she could have bitten her tongue out.

'Hanging on Karina's words?' Rick sounded surprised and amused. 'Lucy, are you jealous?'

'Certainly not. I couldn't care less who you flirt with.' She pulled away from him, angry with him and with herself.

'I wasn't flirting with her.'

'No?' She shrugged. 'Well, as I said, I really couldn't care.'

'Karina is just a friend now, Lucy.'

'Fine.' Lucy nodded and stared straight ahead. 'She still seems very fond of you.' She added the words as an afterthought in case she sounded too abrupt.

'Well, I'm fond of her.'

'It's nice when a relationship can end in a civilised manner.'

'You and Kris seem pretty civilised about things,' Rick said quietly.

'It's a veneer for work.' Lucy shrugged. 'I didn't feel civilised when he left. I wanted to throw all his clothes out of the window and get John Layton to sack him.'

Rick laughed at that. 'I can't imagine you doing anything like that. Are you sure you're not a fire sign?'

Lucy smiled. 'Well, I didn't do anything like that,' she added hurriedly. 'I just felt like it.'

'Understandable under the circumstances.'

'Doesn't make you feel good about yourself, though.' Lucy shrugged. 'Dark thoughts like that can destroy you.'

'That's what almost destroyed my father,' Rick said grimly. 'He was very bitter and quite twisted for a number of years after his divorce.'

Lucy shivered. 'I'm glad I didn't go there.'

'So you don't want me to sack Kris, then?' Rick smiled.

'No.' Lucy flicked an amused glance up at him, unsure if he was joking or not. 'But thanks for the offer.'

'Are you going to phone him?'

'Eventually.' She shrugged. 'Maybe when I get back to Barbados.'

'I think he wants you back.'

'Back in London?' She frowned.

'Back in his life.'

The quiet observation made her laugh. 'You must be joking. Really, I assure you, Rick, he's happy. He's probably much more suited to Sandra than he ever was to me. John is right, it's more likely to be the job out here that he's after.'

'Yes, well, he's definitely not having that,' Rick said firmly. 'So what about you and me? Do you want to give it a whirl?'

The conversation's sudden change in direction took her by surprise. 'I thought you weren't going to rush me?' she hedged.

'I didn't think I was.' His lips twisted wryly. 'But as I told you, I am not the most patient of men. And I want you back in my bed.' He added the words huskily and the way he said them, the way he looked at her, made her body catch fire.

Maybe she should just throw caution away, Lucy thought hazily as she looked up into his eyes. She wanted him so much, and could she get any more hurt than she would be right at this moment if she threw everything away?

'Rick, I—'

A couple walking around the deck interrupted them. It was John Layton and his wife, and they came over to stand beside them. 'Isn't it beautiful out here?' John said with a smile.

'Absolutely,' Lucy agreed. She wasn't sure if she was

glad of the interruption or sorry, because she had been going to say yes to Rick...

'I'm going to get John to take me on a fourteen-day cruise as soon as he retires,' his wife said dreamily. 'It's so romantic.'

'Well, we'll leave you two in peace.' John put his arm through his wife's and tried to lead her away, but she was in full flow of conversation.

'At first when John told me he was retiring, I was very taken aback and not pleased at all. But now I'm coming around to the idea, I'm feeling better about it.'

'I didn't know you were retiring, John?' Lucy said in surprise.

John shrugged. 'Nothing lasts for ever. You've got to embrace change.'

The words echoed peculiarly inside Lucy and before she could make any kind of a reply the couple were moving away on their amble around the deck.

'I didn't know John was leaving.' Lucy looked over at Rick. 'Are you forcing him out?'

'What makes you say that?' Rick's voice was suddenly terse.

'Because he didn't sound too pleased to be going.' Lucy stared at him. 'You are, aren't you? You're letting him go!' Suddenly Lucy could feel blood thundering through her veins in fury. 'How could you do that? He's a really decent man!'

'I'm not arguing with that,' Rick said calmly.

'But you've still pushed him out of the company!' Lucy's voice shook.

'I didn't get rid of him, Lucy,' he said quietly. 'And you're very quick to jump to all the wrong conclusions. I've noticed that a few times about you. It's as if you feel it's safer to think badly of me.'

Lucy swallowed down a feeling of panic. There was an

element of truth in those words and the fact that he had hit on it so concisely made her extremely nervous. 'Well, if I jumped to the wrong conclusion I'm sorry.' She murmured the words huskily.

'So why do you do it?' Rick asked coolly.

'Do what?'

'Put up these barriers, usually hastily erected barriers, when we hit anything emotional.'

She glanced up at him uncertainly. 'I don't do that.'

'Yes, you do.'

She shook her head helplessly. She didn't want him to press her like this. 'Well, maybe it just feels safer, okay?' She glared at him.

'Safer?' He frowned.

'Safer than being disappointed in someone later…let down.' She shrugged. 'I don't know, Rick. I just know that in every relationship it's best to keep your eyes open, better to face reality than be a fool.'

'He really did a job on you, didn't he?' Rick replied gruffly.

'Who?' Lucy looked over at him and shook her head. 'This has nothing to do with my ex-husband.'

'Lucy, it has everything to do with him.' Rick's voice was quiet. 'He is the reason why you can't say yes to me, isn't he?'

'No! He's not.' She glared at him.

'Our relationship would be nothing like the one you had with Kris.' Rick said the words softly.

'I know that! I was married to Kris, we made promises…till death do us part, that kind of thing.' Her voice trembled slightly. 'And I took them seriously.'

'I know.' Rick moved closer to her. 'And I know how much he hurt you. But you are going to have to start trusting people again. Not every man is like Kris Bradshaw.'

The words lingered between them.

'I know.' She looked up at him and her eyes shimmered in the moonlight. 'And I'm sorry I jumped to the wrong conclusions…about John.'

'So you should be.' Rick smiled. 'He's decided himself that he wants early retirement; he says he wants to spend more time on the golf course and with his grandchildren.'

Lucy nodded. 'It was just a shock, that's all.'

'So shall we kiss and make up, or is that against the rules?' Rick asked with a grin.

'Maybe rules are meant to be broken,' Lucy whispered tremulously.

Rick smiled and then gently his lips found hers. It was the sweetest kiss and she stretched her arms up and around his neck, welcoming his touch.

The kiss deepened and inflamed her senses. Nobody had ever turned her on like this with just a kiss.

She loved him so much…too much… The words thundered through her.

Hastily she pulled away. 'We should go inside.'

'Just what I was thinking.' Rick grinned.

'No, Rick, I meant we should circulate. You are supposed to be with your guests.'

'My guests can wait. Besides, half of them are watching a concert.'

Lucy smiled at him. 'And half of them aren't. And that was just a making-up kiss—my old rules still apply.'

'I thought you said rules were meant to be broken.'

'That was under duress. It was a moment of weakness.'

'You know, I think I've met my match with you,' he said with a grin.

'I know you have.' She reached out and took hold of his hand. 'Come on, let's go back inside.'

'Okay…but I want you back in my bed, Lucy. I'll only be patient for so long.'

Lucy smiled. It was taking every ounce of self-control to

keep him at bay. But she felt she needed to take things slowly.

Music was drifting out from one of the lounges and they followed the sound.

Karina was standing at the bar with a group of people, but as soon as she saw Rick she detached herself and came towards them.

'Before I forget, Rick. We must get together tomorrow to discuss a few details about your father's business. I'm going to fly back to London next month to visit his head office so we need to go over a few things.'

'Yes, we must do that,' Rick said easily. 'I think it will have to be later tomorrow evening, though. My schedule tomorrow is pretty full.'

'That's fine.'

A few people were taking to the dance floor as the band played a romantic ballad.

'Would you like to dance, Lucy?' Rick smiled over at her and she nodded.

Being in Rick's arms had to be the best feeling in the world, she thought dreamily as they danced close together on the crowded floor.

The light touch of his hand against her skin made her tremble inside with need, made her senses soar.

'Do you know what I'm thinking right now?' Rick whispered against her ear.

'End-of-year accounts?' Lucy smiled tremulously up at him.

He laughed. 'That is what I should be thinking of.' His arms tightened around her. 'But instead I'm thinking of all the things I'd like to do to you in bed.'

'You are a terrible tease, Mr Connors.' She smiled and leaned her head against his chest.

'I'm a man with an appetite, Ms Blake.'

The music finished abruptly and reluctantly Lucy broke away from him.

As they walked back to the bar they were engulfed in the crowds. And for the next hour or so they were pitched into conversation with different people.

After a while the buzz of conversation and the smell of alcohol suddenly seemed to make Lucy feel a bit queasy.

Rick glanced across at her. 'You look pale suddenly.'

'I'm fine, just a bit tired. I think I'll turn in.'

Rick nodded and reached to kiss her on the cheek.

Then he watched as she made her way out of the lounge, and it took all his self-control not to follow her. But he sensed if he didn't take this slowly he would lose her.

CHAPTER TWELVE

As LUCY lay in bed she could feel the ship moving gently up and down. It was a bit like being lulled to sleep on a hammock. She closed her eyes and thought back over the day.

There was a part of her that wished she had invited Rick back to her bed. But she was right to take this slowly, she told herself, trying very hard to be sensible. She agreed that it was time she learned to trust again. However she had already made one mistake in the past, thinking she knew Kris when really she hadn't. And if you didn't learn from the mistakes of the past there wasn't much hope for the future. No man would ever make a fool of her again.

It was strange how exhausted she felt, she thought, rolling over onto her side. And that feeling of sickness—that was strange too, but she supposed that could be down to the movement of the ship. She closed her eyes and fell into a deep sleep.

Lucy woke up several hours later. The room was still pitch black and through the window she could see the moon reflecting on the water. She felt incredibly thirsty. Sleepily she reached for her dressing gown and wandered through to the lounge to get a glass of water from the mini bar.

As she brought her drink back to bed she noticed that the door to Rick's cabin was ajar and the light was on in there. It swung open a little wider as the ship moved. And she had a clear view of Rick's bed. It was empty and still perfectly made.

Lucy frowned and glanced at her watch. It was two-thirty.

But then that was probably early on a ship. In all likelihood he was in the casino or talking with friends in the bar.

As she headed back to bed she suddenly felt a bit queasy again. The feeling was really quite odd. She had never suffered from travel sickness of any form in her life.

She finished the glass of water and lay down.

The next thing Lucy knew, sunlight was dazzling in through the window. She blinked and rubbed her eyes. A tropical island shimmered on the blue horizon. The hills were green and lush and palm trees fringed a white beach. It looked so beautiful that for a moment she just lay there drinking it in.

She felt okay this morning, so she must just have been overtired last night. Reaching for her dressing gown, she headed to have a shower.

It was as she walked towards the bathroom that the sickness struck again without warning. And this time it was so vicious that she had to run the last few steps, slamming the door behind her.

What on earth was wrong with her? As with yesterday morning, it took a while for the feeling to pass, but when it did she felt absolutely fine again.

She showered and changed into a pale blue dress that was summery and yet stylish. And after a few moments' attention on her hair and make-up, she looked almost radiant. She even felt hungry. So whatever it was that was wrong with her, it couldn't be serious.

When she stepped out into the lounge she was surprised to see the doors onto the balcony were open and Rick was sitting outside at a table laid for two, drinking a cup of coffee.

'Morning.' He stood up as soon as he saw her. 'How did you sleep?'

'Very well, thank you.' She smiled at him, feeling suddenly shy as she remembered some of their conversation last night, and the way he had held her on the dance floor.

She took the seat opposite and lifted up the menu on the table. 'What about you?'

'Well, eventually I slept...' She caught the gleam of amusement in his eye. 'I had a nightcap out on deck and it helped.'

'So what are the plans for today?' she asked briskly, thinking it was probably safer to focus on work, not on anything personal.

'Well, Grenada is beckoning. So at some point we should go ashore—'

'Yes, but don't forget you've got to give some interviews today to the journalists you've invited. They are scheduled for...' Lucy reached for her bag and got out her diary. 'Ah, yes, one-thirty. Then we're supposed to be meeting James Donaldson to discuss the Miami marketing plan...'

'What would I do without you, Lucy?' Rick grinned. 'You really are very efficient.'

'That's why you've brought me out here,' she said lightly, then glanced over at him with a frown. 'And are you being facetious?' she asked as an afterthought.

'No, Lucy.' He laughed. 'I was actually being serious. Although I have to say that your efficiency isn't the only reason I want you out here...' He murmured the words and she felt herself go hot all over in response.

Not wanting to give him the pleasure of seeing how easily he could embarrass her, she pretended to be deeply engrossed in the notes she had made at the back of her diary. 'Oh, and there's the presentation at twelve for the head of the sales team in Miami as well.'

He didn't answer her immediately and she flicked a curious glance across at him.

'Presentation at twelve.' He nodded seriously, but she could still see a hint of humour in his dark eyes.

He really could be quite infuriating, she thought. But he was also extremely attractive. She flicked another look across at him. He was dressed in a short-sleeved khaki shirt and lightweight trousers. She couldn't help noticing the strength of the muscles in his arms, the breadth of his shoulders.

Speedily she wrenched her gaze away from him as a steward arrived to ask if she'd like to order something for breakfast.

'Yes, please. I'll have the grapefruit, followed by cream cheese and smoked salmon bagels, and some orange juice, and can I have a glass of water? Thank you.'

She looked over to find Rick regarding her with some amusement. 'For a woman who said she doesn't eat breakfast, you're doing okay today.'

'Yes, it's pretty weird, actually.' She smiled, somewhat surprised herself. 'Especially as I felt a little bit seasick this morning.'

'Seasick!' Rick sounded amused.

'What's so funny about that?'

'Nothing.' He grinned at her. 'It's just that the sea is as calm as a millpond and apart from that there are enough stabilisers on this ship to make a force-ten storm feel tranquil.'

'Well, I must just be the sensitive type,' she said with a shrug.

'Yes, you must.'

'Anyway.' Lucy picked up her diary again and wished she hadn't told him that. She didn't want him to think she was weak; on the contrary, she wanted him to know that she was strong and capable. Firmly she concentrated on the day ahead. 'So, as I was saying, you have quite a busy schedule today.'

'Yes, I know.' Rick reached for the coffee pot. 'Would you like a cup?'

Lucy shook her head, her stomach protesting suddenly at the very thought of coffee.

'Oh, and I was also wondering if I should organise a leaving present for John Layton. We should mark the event in some way,' she said briskly.

'That is a good idea. But maybe we should do that back in London with the other staff. He's leaving the ship early tomorrow morning, because he and his wife are having a week's holiday on Antigua.'

Lucy nodded. 'Okay, I'll arrange it when I get home.'

The steward brought in the food she had ordered and there was silence for a while.

'So what should we do?' Rick asked as they were left alone again.

'I suppose we could get him a watch, although it's not very original.'

'Not about John Layton, about us,' Rick said quietly.

'Oh!' She looked across at him in surprise and as she met the darkness of his eyes her body seemed to pulse with adrenalin. How easy it would be to just say: yes, I want to come to Barbados; I want you to take me back to bed. It was what she wanted to say. But then the sensible side of her was saying: don't rush…be careful…

'I don't know, Rick,' she murmured. 'I need more time.'

'I thought a good night's sleep might have sufficed.'

Lucy shook her head. Then in an attempt to change the subject she glanced out over the sea towards the island. 'I take it that's Grenada?'

'Yes. If you close your eyes and take a deep breath you can smell the spices from here.'

Lucy did as he asked. She could smell the salt in the air but also a hint of warm spice. 'Nutmeg and cinnamon,' she guessed.

Rick watched her, watched the way the sun gleamed over

her hair highlighting the gold and bronze lights in it. She was incredibly beautiful.

'Lucy, I—'

'Oh, and before I forget,' she cut across him quickly. 'You have two meetings scheduled with someone called Brian Dawn. I came across some of the notes as I was flicking through those papers you gave me—'

'Lucy.' He cut across her firmly. 'Let's forget work for a moment, shall we?'

Lucy looked across and met his eyes. 'Let's not, Rick,' she answered with equal firmness. 'Today is Monday and as far as I'm concerned it's business as usual.'

Rick didn't look amused.

He liked business on his terms, she realised suddenly. He liked to dictate the pace. Well, he was going to have to just step back because, like it or not, she was going to dictate the pace with this.

There was a knock on the door and Karina walked in. She looked very attractive in a short skirt and clinging white top, almost as if she were off to play a game of tennis. 'Good morning.' She smiled at them both.

'Come and join us.' Rick pulled out a chair.

'Have you recovered yet?' Karina asked him and he grinned.

'Recovered from what?' Lucy asked.

'Oh, hasn't he told you?' Karina laughed. 'He was sitting out on deck with me last night, drinking.'

'Just one drink.' Rick smiled. 'And as I recall it was you who downed the rest of that champagne.'

'Yes, I have to admit, my head is pounding. I could do with some sunglasses, actually. You don't have a pair I could borrow, do you, Rick? I can't find mine.'

'I think I have a spare pair.' Lucy stood up. 'I'll go and have a look.'

When she returned Karina was leaning across the table smiling at Rick in an openly flirtatious way.

Lucy sat back down and handed her the glasses. 'Thank you, Lucy.' The woman smiled at her. 'Well, I'll run along…and I'll see you later, Rick.'

Then she was gone.

'I thought she was going to stay and have coffee,' Lucy said casually.

'She's booked on a trip around the island. I think it leaves at nine-thirty.'

Lucy nodded. 'Well I suppose I should get on myself,' she said briskly, not wanting to dwell on Karina Stockwell. Maybe the woman did still fancy Rick, but the relationship was finished and she was married, Lucy told herself firmly. 'I need to start going through those papers on your desk.'

Rick caught hold of her hand as she made to turn away. 'How about we have dinner together on Grenada tonight?' he asked softly. 'I know a nice little restaurant that is very secluded with wonderful views of the bay.'

Lucy hesitated and then smiled at him. 'Sounds wonderful.'

As the day wore on Lucy organised and sorted through a number of marketing plans. She chatted to the journalists and organised coffee and snacks to be served in the cabin whilst they were interviewing Rick. And then later she went up on deck to see how the entertainment on board was going.

A steel band was playing by the pool and a few people were lying on sunbeds, some sitting in the shade. There was a relaxed lazy atmosphere and the heat was intense.

'I think you've done enough for one day,' Rick said as he came through and saw her sitting in the shade for a moment. 'When I said I wanted you to help me with things, I didn't mean for you to work this hard. You haven't stopped all day.'

'I'm fine.'

'Take some time off,' Rick said firmly. 'Take a dip in the pool.'

Lucy looked over towards the water. It did look inviting. 'Maybe I will.'

He reached out and stroked a hand across her cheek. The gesture was so exquisitely tender that it made her heart turn over.

'Okay, I'll see you later.' He smiled at her and walked away.

Lucy leaned back against the sun lounger and closed her eyes. Love was such a strange emotion, she thought wryly. Such small gestures could bring such intense highs…

'Afternoon, Lucy.' She opened one eye and saw Karina standing over her.

'Hi, how's the hangover?' Lucy asked with a smile.

'It's much better. I've brought your sunglasses back for you.' Karina put them down beside her and then pulled out a chair at the table and beckoned to a passing waiter. 'Would you like a drink, Lucy?'

'Yes, okay, I'll have an orange juice.'

'Very virtuous.' Karina smiled. 'I'll have a vodka and tonic,' she told the waiter.

'Hair of the dog?' Lucy said with a smile.

'Something like that.'

'It's a pity your partner couldn't make this trip,' Lucy said casually, stretching her legs out into the sun. 'Is he working?'

'Yes. He's always working.' Karina shrugged.

Lucy frowned and wondered why she felt as if she had just stepped on a minefield. 'How did you enjoy the island tour?' she asked, changing the subject.'

'It was interesting,' Karina said with a nod.

The waiter brought their drinks.

Lucy searched around for some more light conversation, but nothing much presented itself.

'So what is Rick doing this afternoon?' Karina asked suddenly.

'He's got a meeting with James Donaldson.'

'Ah, yes.' Karina sipped her drink. 'You are very capable, Lucy,' she added wryly. 'Everyone says that about you.'

'Do they?' Lucy shrugged. 'Well, I enjoy my job.'

'Yes. Which makes you very much Rick's type. He loves intelligent, beautiful women who are an asset to his business.'

'Well, I'll take that as a compliment, Karina, thanks.'

Karina nodded and stood up. 'Just be very careful not to read too much into it,' she said softly. 'Because, believe me, getting serious about Rick is a big mistake. That's the moment when he cuts the ties.'

Lucy sat up and looked at the other woman. 'Thanks for the advice,' she said coolly. 'But I don't really need it.'

'No, of course not.' The other woman gave her a brittle smile. 'Well, I'll see you later.'

Lucy's blood was pounding through her veins as she leaned back against the chair again. How dared the woman say that to her? She had a real nerve… And what would she know about her relationship with Rick? Maybe he'd be different with her from how he'd been with Karina.

And maybe she was kidding herself. The words crept in, unwelcome, unwanted.

Lucy stood up. She didn't feel like a swim now. Instead she took her drink and returned to her cabin.

It was cool and pleasant inside. Lucy finished her drink and then wandered through and did some more paperwork at Rick's desk. Keeping her mind occupied helped. She didn't want to think about Karina's words; they were too upsetting, especially as she knew deep down that they were probably true.

Falling in love with Rick was doubtless a big mistake. A leopard didn't change his spots. And she could get badly hurt. But on the other hand maybe it would work out. If she didn't at least give it a go, wouldn't she always wonder what might have been?

The shrill ring of the phone coming from her cabin made her jump. Hurriedly she went to answer it. She half expected it to be Rick asking her why she wasn't lazing by the pool. Instead she was surprised and delighted to hear Mel's cheerful tones.

'Hi there, I thought I'd ring you from cold, rainy, miserable London and ask how things are.'

'Things are fine.' Lucy took the phone and sat down on her bed. 'It's so lovely to hear your voice.'

'Really? Things mustn't be *that* good, then. Listen, I won't stay on too long because this will cost me a fortune. But I just wanted to tell you a bit of gossip that's all over the office.'

'What's that?' Lucy asked curiously.

'Kris and his girlfriend have split.'

'Split!' Lucy was astounded. 'No, you've got that wrong. They're having a baby, Mel.'

'No, Sandra is having a baby…but it's not Kris's.'

For a moment Lucy was so dumbfounded she couldn't speak. 'Poor Kris,' she said eventually.

'Serves him right, you mean!' Mel spluttered.

Lucy shook her head. The strange thing was that she did feel sorry for Kris and, considering how angry and upset she had felt regarding that baby, her reaction surprised her. She wondered if it meant that finally she had left the past behind her and had moved on.

'Anyway, I had to tell you,' Mel continued cheerfully. 'Now I'd better go. Hope all is hot and steamy with you?'

'It is certainly hot.'

'Lucky thing, but hope it's steamy too. Just remember you are young, free and single—enjoy yourself!'

Lucy was still smiling as she put the phone down. Mel was such a breath of fresh air.

And she was right. Life was for living. She would take a chance on Rick, see where it led. She'd say yes to him tonight.

The door into the cabin opened and Rick walked in. 'Hello, I didn't expect to see you down here.'

'I thought I'd finish that paperwork, and then have a shower, ready for tonight.'

Rick's eyes moved to the telephone in her hand. 'Been phoning someone?'

Lucy shook her head. 'No.'

'Good.' He murmured the word in an absent fashion as he walked over towards his desk. 'You haven't seen that file that I earmarked for Miami, have you?'

'It's in the third drawer down.' She watched as he opened the drawer and found the document.

'Thanks.' He shot a glance over at her. 'What would I do without you?' he said with a grin. 'I'll see you later. I've got to get back; people are waiting for me.'

Lucy nodded.

When he left she walked back to the desk and tried to continue with her work.

What would I do without you? That was the second time today that Rick had joked like that.

But of course the truth was that he would do very well without her. Rick didn't need anyone.

She would just have to make herself even more indispensable, then, she thought firmly. And make him fall in love with her.

Her mind filled with Rick and their relationship, Lucy picked up her bag. She intended to fill a few dates in her diary from some lists Rick had left her. But as she flicked through the pages a red star caught her eye. She usually marked the first day of her period in her diary with a red star. The date was the fifth of January. There were no other red stars after it.

Lucy stared at the pages and then frantically started to count.

CHAPTER THIRTEEN

LUCY watched a moth fluttering around the candle on the table. It was tiny, but it keep determinedly fluttering and diving towards the flame.

It was a bit like her, Lucy thought. One moment full of bravado, the next almost giving up, then back for another try…

'Would you like a cognac with your coffee?' Rick asked her. She glanced across at him distractedly.

They were in an old-world restaurant up in the Grenada rainforest, and it was probably the most romantic place Lucy had ever visited. Its floors were uneven; the windows had no glass, just blue shutters opened wide to reveal a spectacular view down towards the bay of St George where their ship was moored. Now darkness had fallen and the lights below twinkled invitingly. The *Contessa* looked like a toy ship, its light reflecting like molten gold over the water.

But Lucy couldn't enjoy anything: not the surroundings, not the fabulous food, not even her handsome companion across the table from her. Because she was too busy trying not to think about what could be causing her bouts of illness.

'No, I'll just have coffee, thank you.' She smiled across at him.

Was she pregnant? With the thought her mind ricocheted back for the umpteenth time to that first night they had shared together in London.

She and Rick had taken precautions that night…so she couldn't be!

But there had been an accident. She hadn't thought anything about it at the time. It wasn't as if it had happened at

174

an absolutely crucial moment…but then all it needed was one slip, one moment.

Lucy swallowed down a feeling of absolute disbelief. This was all in her imagination. Okay, her period was late…very late. But that could just be down to a glitch with her body clock.

'You've been very quiet tonight,' Rick said casually. 'And you haven't touched your wine.'

'I think the heat is getting to me.' She smiled over at him. 'But I shouldn't complain, should I? Not when it's raining and cold in London.'

'How do you know that it's raining and cold in London?'

Rick's eyes flicked over her and he noticed how the colour on her creamy skin heightened immediately.

'Isn't it always?' she said lightly. Lucy didn't want to start talking about Mel's phone call because that would only lead to talking about Kris. And frankly she was tired of that subject. She wasn't even going to phone him. Whatever he wanted, it would have to wait until she was back home.

The waitress brought their coffee and Lucy tried to relax back into the ambiance of the place.

'It's been a lovely evening, Rick. Thank you.'

Rick's gaze seemed very intense. 'I'm glad you enjoyed it.'

What should she say if he asked her for a decision? she wondered in panic. She could hardly say yes now.

Rick had made it very clear that he only wanted an affair with her. He wasn't a man who wanted to settle down and make a commitment, and wasn't a baby the biggest commitment of all?

She cleared her throat nervously. This was all hypothetical, because she didn't even know for certain if she was pregnant. But there was a way to find out, she thought suddenly. There was a doctor on board the ship. She had sat next to him last night at dinner.

'What time do we sail tonight?' she asked Rick.

'Nine-thirty.'

She pushed her coffee away from her slightly. The freshly ground smell, which she had once adored, seemed to be cloying and heavy, and she really didn't want it.

'Shall we go?' Rick asked her quietly and she nodded.

Rick put a hand up and the waitress brought the bill.

The drive in the taxi back down to the ship was made almost in silence. Rick put an arm around her and she allowed herself to lean her head against his shoulder. The breeze through the open windows was laced with cinnamon. She would always remember the Spice Island as the place where she thought she was pregnant. Lucy closed her eyes and allowed herself to dream that it was true and she was expecting a baby. A flutter of excitement stirred inside her. She imagined telling Rick…imagined that he was pleased. And a thrill of happiness swept through her.

But deep down she knew she was deluding herself. Rick wouldn't be pleased.

What was it Karina had said? *Getting serious about Rick is a big mistake. That's the moment when he cuts the ties.*

The taxi pulled up at the dockside and they got out. 'I almost forgot. I bought you something,' Rick said suddenly as they walked hand in hand towards the gangplank. He let go of her and reached into his pocket to bring out a small purple wristband.

'What is it?' she asked curiously.

'You wear it on your wrist and it's supposed to cure sea-sickness.'

Lucy laughed. 'I'll give it a try. Thank you.'

Rick took hold of her hand and gently he put it on for her. 'There.' The touch of his hands against her skin sent little darts of awareness racing through her. He looked into her eyes. 'I hope it helps. Because I don't want anything upsetting you, Lucy…' He reached out and traced a hand down over the side of her face.

Suddenly she wanted to cry. He was so sweet and so kind and she wanted more than anything to just go into his arms and tell him she was his…but she couldn't do that. She couldn't, because if she was pregnant, the relationship would be over.

Lucy pulled away from him. 'Better get back on board,' she said brightly.

'Yes.' He took hold of her hand again and they walked up towards the security check. 'We are in Antigua tomorrow. And as all the work is done we can relax and just enjoy ourselves. I'll take you to Nelson's Dockyard. It's worth a visit.'

Lucy tried to concentrate on what he was saying, but all she could think was that she needed to find out for certain one way or another if she was pregnant, and she needed to find out tonight.

'Shall we have a drink up on deck?' Rick asked her.

'Yes, good idea…but you go on ahead. I just want to change out of this dress.'

'What's wrong with your dress?' Rick asked in amusement, his eyes sweeping over the stylish black number. 'You look beautiful.'

'I just thought I'd put something else on.' She moved away from him towards the lifts. 'I won't be long. I'll see you up on deck.'

She knew the medical centre was at the back of the ship down on a lower floor. But it took her a while to find it and when she did it seemed to be deserted. Her heart plummeted. Lucy was just turning back when a nurse put her head out from an office door. 'Can I help you?'

'I hope so.' Lucy smiled at her. 'Can I come in?'

It was early morning and the ship was docking in Antigua. Lucy sat by the window in her cabin and looked out. Her bags were packed and on the dressing table there was a note for Rick. A note that apologised for leaving without telling him or saying goodbye, and thanking him for his offer of a job in Barbados—an offer she could not take. She hadn't given him any reasons.

Lucy bit down on her lip. She couldn't tell him that she was pregnant. It would be naïve in the extreme to think he would want the baby. And the thing was, *she* did. In fact she wanted this baby with all of her heart.

After the doctor had told her that the test was positive she had spent the whole night thinking about her situation.

If she decided to go ahead with the pregnancy she would not only lose Rick, but also her job in London. There was no way she could stay on there. Everyone would talk and the news would get back to Rick and he would do his sums and he would know that he was the father...

Knowing Rick, he would probably try and do the honourable thing by her, which in his case would mean money, not commitment or involvement.

She didn't want that. It was too painful. She'd rather be independent. And she was sure she would manage on her own. The thought of her baby was what spurred her on. She wanted a child so much that the momentous decision she had made at midnight to give up her job, sell her flat and move away to the country hadn't been that difficult. The money from her flat would be enough to pay for somewhere small and buy her some time to find another job.

But in the meantime her priority was to get away from here—from Rick—because if she saw him it would break her heart. Better to just leave a note and concentrate on practicalities, on things she could fix, not on things she couldn't have. She loved Rick so much that it hurt, but she had to be realistic.

From outside in the corridor she could hear the announcement that the ship had docked and the gangplanks were down for anyone who wanted to disembark.

There was a tap on the outer door that led direct from her cabin to the corridor. It would be the porter for her luggage.

CHAPTER FOURTEEN

LONDON was grey and cold and it seemed to match her mood. Lucy was exhausted both physically and emotionally.

Because she would have had to hang around the airport in Antigua for ten hours before she could get on a direct flight to London, Lucy had opted for a flight to Barbados that left immediately and had spare seats. This had then been linked immediately with a direct flight back to London. It had got her home quicker than waiting around in Antigua but she felt as if she had been travelling for ever, and although she was tired she hadn't been able to sleep on the plane. Her mind had been going over and over things.

What would Rick think when he got her note? Would he be angry? Or would he just shrug and forget about her?

The taxi pulled up outside her flat.

It was starting to rain now and the streets were misty and dark. She found her front-door key and stepped out of the car. The driver lifted her bag out of the boot and with a wave he drove away.

'What took you so long?'

The familiar voice made her whirl around.

It was a shock to see Rick stepping out from a car parked behind her. For a moment she thought she was imagining things, hallucinating. Maybe she wanted to see him so badly that her mind was playing tricks.

He walked closer towards her. It wasn't a dream—he really was here. Her heart lurched with joy and fear and a mixture of emotions so sharp and poignant she couldn't think straight. 'What are you doing here?' she whispered huskily.

'I was going to ask you the same question.'

He sounded cool and calm.

'Did you get my note?' Her voice wavered slightly.

It was raining harder now. Rick watched as it slanted over her, soaking her long hair. 'Let's discuss this inside, Lucy.' Calmly he reached out and picked up her suitcase for her.

Lucy hesitated. She supposed she had to let him in, and he did deserve some kind of explanation for her disappearance, but she didn't know what to say to him. She hadn't expected this. She felt unprepared, out of her depth…

Rick took her front-door key from her and with a grim look of determination he preceded her into the house.

Everything in her flat looked exactly the same and yet it felt different to her. She felt different, as if she had left as one person and arrived back as someone else. It was a weird feeling.

Rick took his jacket off and bent to light the fire. And suddenly it was as if nothing had changed, and she was transported back to that night after the speed dating when she had invited him in. The night she had slept with him…the night that had changed the whole course of her life.

She took off her coat and hung it behind the door. Her hands were trembling.

'So why did you run away?' Rick turned to face her.

'I didn't run away.' She raised her head in that determined way that Rick recognised so well, but he could see the shadows in her eyes.

'That's exactly what you did, Lucy,' he said softly. 'Was it because of Kris?'

'Kris?' She frowned.

'Come on, Lucy. I know he rang you when you were on board the ship in Grenada—'

'He didn't!'

'Yes, he did, and he told you his relationship was at an

end and that he wanted you back. That's the reason you were so quiet when we went out to dinner...the reason you retired to your cabin and told me you were tired. The reason you ran back here.'

'No!' Her voice broke slightly. 'You've got it all wrong!'

Rick shook his head. 'No, I haven't. You still love him, don't you?'

She shook her head.

'You're a fool if you go back to him, Lucy,' Rick continued firmly and he took another few steps closer. 'He'll hurt you again. You can't trust him.'

He looked down into her eyes and noticed how brightly they shimmered. 'Please don't go back to him, Lucy...'

The soft, husky words tore into her and she had to swallow down on a knot of tears in her throat. 'I'm not going to go back to him.'

Rick held her gaze steadily. 'So you'll come back to Barbados with me?' The question was put quite firmly.

She shook her head.

'Why not?'

She bit down on her lip. 'I just can't...' She whispered the words unsteadily.

'That's not good enough, Lucy. I want a reason.'

The silence stretched between them.

'I want you...' he said softly.

Her heart was thundering against her chest now. This was just too much for her to bear. She loved him so much, wanted him so much...

'It just wouldn't work out, Rick.' She forced herself to say the words, but a tear trickled down her face.

'Yes, it would. I'll make it work.' He said the words firmly. Then he reached and wiped her tears away with a gentle hand. 'Because I love you, Lucy. I love you with all my heart.'

Lucy looked up at him, astonished. She could hardly believe he had said those words to her. Her heart missed several beats.

'Don't say that, Rick.' She whispered the words unsteadily, and then she shook her head. 'You just want me to fill the space in your bed, but you don't really love me...'

'Yes, I want you to fill the space in my bed.' He said the words gently. 'But I also want you to fill the space in my life, because without you my life is empty. I love you more than I can tell you.'

Tears started to pour down her cheeks now.

'Please don't cry.' He wiped the tears away soothingly. 'I know you're scared of making a mistake, Lucy, and I know you still have feelings for Kris—'

'I *don't* have any feelings for Kris.' She said the words sternly but her voice was raw with tears. 'You've got it all wrong. I didn't speak to him on the phone. I haven't given him more than a passing thought in ages.'

'So why did you run away?'

'I just couldn't stay.'

'But we were getting on well together. I feel we belong together...can't you feel it?'

She shook her head helplessly.

'Lucy...' He tipped her face upwards and then he kissed her. It was such a tender, loving kiss that it took her breath away; it made her dizzy with need...it made her sway closer and kiss him back, pouring all her heart into that caress.

'There. Can't you feel how right this is?' Rick murmured the words huskily as he lifted his head. 'I knew it the first moment I kissed you...' He stroked her hair back from her face. 'The first moment I held you. And I've tried not to rush things, tried not to scare you away. I thought if I could just get you to Barbados and take things slowly from there, that one day you would start to trust me. That one day you might agree to become my wife.'

Lucy pulled back slightly from him. 'Now I know I'm

hallucinating.' She whispered the words in a dazed tone. 'Aren't you the man who is commitment phobic, the man who puts business first and wants no ties?'

'I used to be that man, before I met you.' Rick smiled at her. 'But I realise now that I was like that because I just hadn't met the right woman. I needed to be sure and there were always doubts with every other woman. It was easy to put business first and dedicate myself to my career. But now...' He stroked her hair back from her face and pulled her closer. 'Now I want so much more. I know without any doubt that you are the right woman, and I want you so much it hurts.'

Lucy smiled up at him tremulously. She felt as if this were some kind of a dream and she would wake at any moment and find that she was still on that plane circling over London. 'I think you might get more than you bargained for with me,' she murmured.

'Oh, I know that.' He smiled. 'That's one of the things I love about you.'

Lucy moved back from him. 'So, let me get this right...when you asked me to be your mistress you really wanted me as your wife?'

Rick nodded. 'I thought if I told you exactly what was in my heart you'd run a mile. But you seem to have run a few miles anyway.' His lips twisted wryly. 'So much for Plan A.'

'So this is Plan B, is it?' She smiled at him. 'Follow me back to London and put your cards on the table?'

He nodded. 'I'm not going to take no for an answer, Lucy. If you don't want to live in Barbados, then I'll just have to move to London.'

'You'd do that for me?'

'I'd do anything for you,' he said softly.

'Then maybe I'd better put my cards on the table as well.' Lucy took a deep breath. 'Rick, the reason I came home so abruptly was that I discovered I was pregnant. I'm going to have your baby.'

The words fell into a deep silence. She could see the shock on his face. He was totally dumbfounded.

'I know this changes things.' She said the words unsteadily. 'And don't worry, I don't expect anything from you,' she added hastily. 'Just because you say you love me doesn't mean I'm going to hold you to anything—'

'You're pregnant?' He was still staring at her blankly.

She nodded. 'I only found out yesterday.'

'And you weren't going to tell me?' His eyes narrowed on her.

'I didn't think you were serious about me.' Her voice sounded raw now. 'And I didn't want you to feel obligated in any way... I knew you weren't into commitment, so—'

'So you thought you'd just run away and not tell me.' He sounded angry now.

Lucy swallowed hard. 'It wasn't what I wanted to do. But I didn't think I had a choice...you never said anything about loving me...' Her eyes suddenly filled with tears.

'Oh, God, Lucy, don't cry.' He took hold of her and then led her over towards the sofa. 'Come on, sit down...you shouldn't be getting upset, not in your condition, and you shouldn't be in those wet clothes either.'

'Rick, stop fussing,' she murmured.

'Someone needs to fuss over you.' Rick headed into the bathroom and came back with a towel. 'You've just flown halfway around the world, you look exhausted and you need to take care of yourself.' He sat down beside her. 'I need to take care of you.' He amended the words firmly.

She glanced across at him sharply. 'No, you don't. I can manage on my own.'

Rick looked at her with a raised eyebrow. 'You are not on your own, Lucy,' he said softly. 'So you don't have to *manage*, as you put it. You do want this baby, don't you?' he asked suddenly.

She noticed how pale and tense he looked as he waited for her reply.

'Yes, of course I want it,' she said huskily.

He raked a hand through the darkness of his hair and the look of relief on his face was very evident. 'Thank heavens for that.'

She looked over at him hesitantly. 'So you don't mind that I'm pregnant?'

'Mind?' He shook his head. 'No, I don't mind. I'm just overwhelmed.'

'You don't have to stay with me just because I'm pregnant.' She put the towel down.

'Lucy, have you been listening to anything I've said?' he murmured quietly, his eyes holding steadily with hers. 'I love you.'

'I know what you said...' Her voice trembled. 'But a baby changes things.'

'Yes, a baby makes this even more special.' He pulled her around and reached to kiss her.

She kissed him back, her lips trembling beneath his.

'I love you so much, Lucy.' He put a hand on her stomach. 'And I'll love our baby very much. And I want to look after you and protect you and be with you for ever more.'

She started to cry again. 'Sorry, it must be my hormones or something.' She wiped the tears away. 'I love you too, Rick.'

'You do!' Rick sat back from her and looked into her eyes.

'Yes, of course I do. I've just been trying to fight it, that's all.'

'Really?' He sounded so amazed, so pleased that she laughed. He pulled her into his arms and held her tightly, then he kissed her again passionately, seductively. 'Tell me that again,' he demanded in a low growl next to her ear.

'I love you, Rick,' she told him steadily. 'I love you more than I've ever loved anyone before.' She glanced up at him. 'Even Kris,' she said firmly.

Rick watched her and smiled. 'And you trust me, then?' She nodded.

'Enough to give marriage one last chance?'

She swallowed hard. 'Yes. Enough to give marriage one final chance.'

He looked at her adoringly. 'And this time it will be for ever,' he promised.

0705/01a

MILLS & BOON®

Live the emotion

Modern
romance™

THE GREEK'S BOUGHT WIFE by Helen Bianchin

Nic Leandros knows that people are only after his money.
So when he finds that beautiful Tina Matheson is pregnant
with his late brother's child, he's certain her price will be
high. Tina must agree to his terms: they will marry for the
baby's sake…

BEDDING HIS VIRGIN MISTRESS by Penny Jordan

Handsome billionaire Ricardo Salvatore is as good at
spending millions as he is at making them, and it's all
for party planner Carly Carlisle. Rumour has it that shy
Carly is his mistress. But the critics say that Carly is just
another woman after his cash…

HIS WEDDING-NIGHT HEIR by Sara Craven

Virginal beauty Cally Maitland has become accustomed to
life on the run since fleeing her marriage to Sir Nicholas
Tempest. But Nicholas isn't prepared to let Cally go.
He has a harsh ultimatum: give him their long-overdue
wedding night – and provide him with an heir!

THE SICILIAN'S DEFIANT MISTRESS by Jane Porter

Cass can't continue in a relationship that involves just her
body when her heart is breaking. But the deal she made
with Sicilian tycoon Maximos Borsellino was for sex, and
now that isn't enough for Cass he ends the affair. Cass is
distraught – and pregnant…

Don't miss out…
On sale 5th August 2005

*Available at most branches of WHSmith, Tesco, ASDA, Martins,
Borders, Eason, Sainsbury's and all good paperback bookshops*

Visit www.millsandboon.co.uk

MILLS & BOON®   0705/01b

Live the emotion

Modern

romance™

IN THE RICH MAN'S WORLD by Carol Marinelli

Budding reporter Amelia Jacobs has got an interview with
billionaire Vaughan Mason. But Vaughan's not impressed
by Amelia. He demands she spend a week with him,
watching him at work – the man whose ruthless tactics in
the bedroom extend to the boardroom!

SANTIAGO'S LOVE-CHILD by Kim Lawrence

Santiago Morais is strong, proud and fiercely passionate
– everything that Lily's husband was not. In his arms
Lily feels awakened. But a shocking discovery convinces
Santiago that Lily has betrayed him, and he sends her away
– not realising that he is the father of her unborn child...

STOLEN BY THE SHEIKH by Trish Morey

Sheikh Khaled Al-Ateeq has granted Sapphire Clemenger
the commission of her dreams: designing the wedding
gown for his chosen bride. Sapphy must accompany the
Prince to his exotic desert palace, and cannot meet his
fiancée. Sapphy doubts that the woman even exists...

THE LAWYER'S CONTRACT MARRIAGE
by Amanda Browning

Samantha Lombardi loved barrister Ransom Shaw. But
she was forced to marry another man to save her family.
Six years on, Sam is widowed and reunited with Ransom.
The sexual pull between them is still strong, and a red-
hot affair ensues. But will Ransom's desire be so easily
satisfied...?

On sale 5th August 2005

*Available at most branches of WHSmith, Tesco, ASDA, Martins,
Borders, Eason, Sainsbury's and all good paperback bookshops*

Visit www.millsandboon.co.uk

MILLS & BOON®

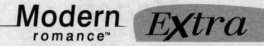

Modern romance™ Extra

More passion for your money!

In August, Mills & Boon Modern Romance is
proud to bring back by popular request,
Raising the Stakes,
and have added a new-in-print linked story,
The Runaway Mistress,
as a bonus. Both come from bestselling,
award-winning author
Sandra Marton.

Sandra has written more than 50 Modern
Romances and her Barons stories have
pleased many readers:

**'An unforgettable read overflowing with
exciting characters, a powerful premise and
smouldering scenes.'**
–Romantic Times

*Available at most branches of WHSmith, Tesco, ASDA, Martins, Borders,
Eason, Sainsbury's and all good paperback bookshops.*

www.millsandboon.co.uk

0705/154

0605/024/MB130

MILLS & BOON

Summer days drifting away...

Summer Loving

VICKI LEWIS THOMPSON
RHONDA NELSON

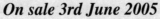

On sale 3rd June 2005

Available at most branches of WHSmith, Tesco, ASDA, Martins, Borders, Eason, Sainsbury's and all good paperback bookshops.

4 FREE

BOOKS AND A SURPRISE GIFT!

We would like to take this opportunity to thank you for reading this Mills & Boon® book by offering you the chance to take FOUR more specially selected titles from the Modern Romance™ series absolutely FREE! We're also making this offer to introduce you to the benefits of the Reader Service™—

- ★ FREE home delivery
- ★ FREE gifts and competitions
- ★ FREE monthly Newsletter
- ★ Exclusive Reader Service offers
- ★ Books available before they're in the shops

Accepting these FREE books and gift places you under no obligation to buy, you may cancel at any time, even after receiving your free shipment. Simply complete your details below and return the entire page to the address below. You don't even need a stamp!

YES! Please send me 4 free Modern Romance books and a surprise gift. I understand that unless you hear from me, I will receive 6 superb new titles every month for just £2.75 each, postage and packing free. I am under no obligation to purchase any books and may cancel my subscription at any time. The free books and gift will be mine to keep in any case.

P5ZED

Ms/Mrs/Miss/Mr ....Initials ....
                                                                    BLOCK CAPITALS PLEASE
Surname ....

Address ....

....

....Postcode.......................................

Send this whole page to:
UK: FREEPOST CN81, Croydon, CR9 3WZ

Offer valid in UK only and is not available to current Reader service subscribers to this series. Overseas and Eire please write for details. We reserve the right to refuse an application and applicants must be aged 18 years or over. Only one application per household. Terms and prices subject to change without notice. Offer expires 31st October 2005. As a result of this application, you may receive offers from Harlequin Mills & Boon and other carefully selected companies. If you would prefer not to share in this opportunity please write to The Data Manager, PO Box 676, Richmond, TW9 IWU.

Mills & Boon® is a registered trademark owned by Harlequin Mills & Boon Limited.
Modern Romance™ is being used as a trademark. The Reader Service™ is being used as a trademark.